The pure adoration and love flowing from these pages and the raw sexual heat was enough to melt my kindle!!! Don't forget the bad guy!!! I loved it so much! I hope to read more of these (hint, hint)!
— SAmbrose

This book is amazing! Julie did a fantastic job with her characters! Her descriptions made it easy to picture myself as the character Olivia, 'Liv' and fall in love with all of the men of her harem! It was hot and erotic and left me wanting to read more of this harem! I hope there are many more books to come about the coven and the harem!
— Stephanie Bockover

The Human and Her Vampires

The Covenant of New Orleans

Book Two

First Edition November 2018

ISBN: 978-1-77357-079-2,

978-1-77357-078-5

Copyright ©2018 by Julie Morgan

Published by: Naughty Nights Press LLC

http://naughtynightspress.com/

Cover Design by: Willsin Rowe

Dedication

For my Gina – thank you for pushing me
past my own limits and pulling stories
you knew were there. I love you!

For my readers, may we be forever
awkward... This story is for you.

Acknowledgements

My Beta Team – where would I be without you? You complete me! Thank you for always supporting. Both Heather's, Melanie, Lisa, both Amanda's, Haylee, Flo, Karlee, and Donna, you ladies are so amazing!!!!!

Debra – I hope you love Tawne's story as much as you did during Penned Con!

Readers – you are why this series has continued. Your love and support are the fuel to continue this project. Look for more news on this series coming soon!

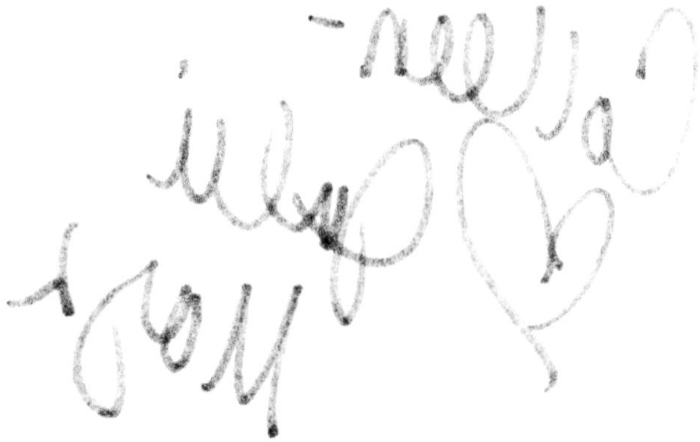

About The Human and Her Vampires

Can dreams become reality...

Tawne O'Brien loves adventure and dreams of living in a world where paranormal creatures exist. Orphaned at a young age, and with a string of failed relationships only adding to her misery, her books are the only salvation from a mundane existence in a universe where she feels completely alone. When her best friend asks her to come visit, her dreams of a new life suddenly become a possibility.

Tawne is introduced to four sexy-as-sin vampires and given the opportunity of a lifetime with no strings attached...or so they say. When she discovers she may only be a guinea pig to the vampires, disappointment regains the upper hand, reminding her of her place in this world.

Can Tawne find the strength inside herself to fight for what she deserves? If she doesn't, she'll lose everything...including any memory of her life with her vampires.

The Human

and

Her Vampires

A Paranormal Reverse
Harem Romance

Julie Morgan

Naughty Nights Press • Canada

Chapter One

A CRISP BREEZE weaved its way through the streets below the indigo sky of New Orleans, Louisiana. The night was clear and the stars flickered in the heavens, as if teasing one another with the mere wink of an eye. The full moon bright as it cast its path along the trees to form unusual shadows on the ground.

It was just before dawn and in the distance of the eastern horizon, the dawn of a new day began.

Tourists would pack the streets

tonight. They would drink their beers, chase one another to see who would end up with the most beads, then head out on a walking tour of vampires in Downtown New Orleans.

And they say it was all just a myth, a part of the city's charm. Although, some days, Tawne O'Brien had hoped for more. She loved the paranormal romance books she read. From being swept up by a star-crossed lover, to finding her soul mate after many reincarnations... But, alas, it was only fiction.

Summer had come to an end around late October. Halloween would be here soon. It was one of Tawne's favorite holidays. Maybe this year she'd dress up as a witch, or a fairy. Maybe a vampire.

She stood out on her deck of her condo on the second floor. The wind blew a gentle breeze around her body. Long tendrils of blonde hair drifted around her shoulders.

Tawne's phone chimed a new text message and vibrated in her pocket. She reached inside and pulled her phone out. A text from Matthew: her current, but soon to be ex, boyfriend. She sighed and rolled her eyes. She'd known early on, during the budding of their relationship, Matthew wasn't the one. He was nice, and one day would make someone happy, but not her.

I want to see you later, the text read.

She had put this off long enough. There was a wall, at least five feet thick, between them, theoretically speaking. She hit reply and began a text.

Listen, we need to talk.

She shook her head, erased the letters on the screen, then tried again.

I think we need to call it quits.

She erased that and tried once more.

Matthew, look, I can't do this anymore. You're great and all, but it's me, not you. I'm not happy. I need to figure out what I need for me, before I can give myself to someone else. I hope you understand.

She hit send. As soon as it was sent, she turned off her phone. He would probably call her, demand an answer, try to talk her out of it, or hell, come over.

She stepped back inside her condo and closed the sliding door behind her. White walls surrounded her with artwork from the local design stores. She crossed the room to her study where her laptop rested open at her wooden corner desk. She sat down and pressed a few keys until the screen flickered out of sleep mode.

The background image displayed Tawne with her parents. An ache in her chest thumped with the beat of her heart. Having died young in an accident not of their own doing took them from her too soon. Her heart ached for a hug from her father, or a kiss on her cheek from her mother. She swiped at a tear that wet her cheek.

Shaking off the sadness, she clicked on the message app. She wanted to send a note over to Olivia, her best friend. They had fallen out of touch with one another. This would be a great time to pick up their friendship.

Olivia had pushed her out of her life when her mother passed away. She knew her friend needed space and time to heal but had not counted on it taking more than a few months.

How long has it been since we talked? A year? Maybe two? Some best friend I am. I've been so self-obsessed with finding someone to date... I'm a bitch.

She began a message to Olivia and started it with, "Well, I'm a seriously nasty bitch. And I love you," when the video app on her computer turned on without warning.

Fuck, don't let it be Matthew. Don't let it be Matthew.

Tawne smiled when she saw Olivia's name flash across the screen. She pressed accept. Olivia's face came into view and Tawne gasped.

"Tawne!" Olivia squealed. "Ohmigawd, it has been too long! Look at you! I love your hair! It's so long!"

Tawne blinked, then chuckled. "Well, I was just starting a message to you, and here you are. Wow, look at you! Whatever you're doing, it's good for you. I haven't seen you look this good, this happy, this... I don't know, glowing? Ever!"

Olivia grinned, and then let out a giggle. A crimson flush crept up her cheeks as she cast her gaze downward.

Tawne lifted a brow. "Okay, spill, who are you seeing and what the hell have you been up to?"

Olivia lifted her gaze back to the monitor and her demeanor calmed. "That's kinda why I was calling. Do you think we could meet up?"

Tawne grinned. "Of course! I'd love to see you. You're my best friend. Tell me when and where."

Her friend nibbled on her finger, then turned to someone talking to her in the distance. Tawne heard a man's voice.

She grinned. "So, who's the mister in the background?"

Olivia turned back to the camera and gave a grin so sly it could melt ice. "We'll talk about that, too. I'm going to message you an address. I'll be there waiting for you."

"This is kinda mysterious," Tawne teased her. "Have you gone into hiding or something?"

Olivia shrugged. "Or something."

The smile on Tawne's lips fell to a frown. "Are you okay?"

"Oh yes! I'm beyond okay. I'm absolutely amazing! My life... Oh, Tawne, I cannot wait to tell you all about it. Just not over the phone, okay?"

Tawne nodded. She wondered if she should go prepared for a fight. She'd heard of men controlling their women and not allowing them to have friends. If this was Olivia's case, she would whip out her bat and her krav maga moves. She had no shame in taking down a man. She would do it if it meant helping out a female in a bad situation.

"All right," Tawne said and sat back in her chair. "I'll see you soon, then. I cannot wait to hug you!"

"Yes!" Olivia squealed again. "I'll see you soon! Muah!" She blew an air kiss into the camera, then the screen went black.

Tawne had always been the quirky one. Feeling awkward in most situations, she became an introverted extrovert. She was quiet until she got to know you. She found herself smiling more often when she was alone in her own thoughts. In her friendship with Olivia, though, it was

Olivia who was down more often than not. It's not that she was a Debbie Downer, but more like she lived a life of depression. It was who she was, and Olivia accepted that about herself. She was alone in the world...just like Tawne. Except for each other, they didn't have anyone else in the world.

Olivia often told her she was the sunshine to the dark storm of her life. As Olivia's best friend, Tawne was there when Olivia lost her mother, and helped her deal with the fall out afterward.

When Olivia left town shortly after, she'd told Tawne that she had to go overseas for some family ceremony. It appeared the family issues were over, and she was back home.

Olivia said she would text the address. For now, that was good enough. She didn't want to turn the phone back on in case Matthew tried calling. She didn't want to deal with voice mails or questions from him. She needed a night out on her own. New movies were at the theater and there was a new action flick staring this hot, up and coming actor.

Tawne grabbed her purse and walked to the bathroom. Facing her reflection in the mirror, she picked up her lip-gloss off the counter. She slid a dab of the light pink gloss over her lips, then tucked the tube into her purse. Satisfied with how she looked, she slipped on her sandals and headed to her front door.

Tonight, would be movie night on her own, with her thoughts. She was ready to find herself. In order to do that, it meant finding happiness as well. She knew that to make it in a relationship, she would have to bring something to the table other than lust and false pretenses of a future she knew she could not provide.

Her parents taught her never to sell herself short and never settle for less than what she deserved. They often reminded her of this, but the last time they did, she'd waved them off with a flick of her hand. If she had known that would be the last time she would see them, talk to them, hug them, she would have taken the time to hug and kiss their cheeks, and tell them how much she loved them.

Olivia was there for her during her emotional outbursts. She'd returned the favor when Olivia had lost her mother.

Tawne pushed the reminiscent thoughts from her mind, closed her apartment door behind her and clicked the thick deadbolt lock into place. Tonight, would be the movies. Tomorrow she'd meet up with Olivia and figure out what she'd been doing overseas, and what the plans were now.

Chapter Two

EXCITEMENT PULSED THROUGH Tawne at the prospect of seeing her best friend again. Olivia became the sister she'd never had. Looking back on their time apart, maybe it was needed. Absence made the heart grow fonder, after all, or something like that.

She slipped her phone from her purse and checked the time. It was close to the time Olivia said she would be at this location. She pulled her texts up once more and verified the location. The directions Olivia sent over had brought Tawne to a dark, warehouse district of New Orleans. It wasn't somewhere she would have picked to meet up. There were no bars, no clubs, no populated buildings of any kind. It was almost frightening.

This is how all horror movies start. In comes the pretty, innocent woman. Then, the dangerous villain creeps up behind her. The woman screams and runs, then trips on an inanimate object only to find herself in the death grip of danger. The spooky, hooded villain hovers above her with a knife.

She rolled her eyes and with a sigh, slid out of her car. The headlights were still on, illuminating the asphalt she stood on. Street lamps glowed a yellow hue in the distance. A shiver slipped down her spine and Tawne pulled her jacket tighter around her body.

In the eerie silence, she only heard her

own shoes strike the ground. Her shadow cast across the lot. Nerves continued to climb, and she considered getting back in her car to drive home.

Why would Olivia want to meet out here, of all places?

She sighed a long breath and as she began to turn toward her car, a hand touched her shoulder. Her heart leapt and Tawne screamed. She whirled around and found Olivia behind her, holding in a giggle.

"You fucking bitch," Tawne growled. "What the hell is wrong with you?"

Olivia held her hand over her lips and shook her head. She wore a red, long-sleeved, v-neck cut top; a black, fitted skirt that ended just above her knees; and black, knee-high boots. She looked amazing. "I'm so sorry. I thought you heard me. Did you not hear me coming?"

"I can't hear anything out here except the beating of my own heart! Why did you scare me like that?"

Olivia opened her mouth, then closed it. "I'll just plead the fifth on that. Now, come here and let me hug you!"

Tawne frowned and lifted a brow. "You realize I owe you a fright now?" She held her arms open and pulled her best friend in for a hug. "I've missed you so much."

"Me too," Olivia whispered. "But, tell me, honestly, am I really that much of a bitch?"

Tawne pulled away and crossed her arms over her chest. "Well, right now, you're up there as *fucking bitch.* Maybe in time, you'll go back to being queen bitch."

Olivia shrugged. "Good enough for me. Come get in my car. We'll have yours brought to my new home. There's a lot I need to catch you up on. Jesse?" Olivia turned around and a young man wearing black, fitted t-shirt and a black hat approached. He stood tall and had a thick build.

Was he her driver? Since when did Olivia have a driver?

"Please, drive Tawne's car home?"

"No problem. Keys?" asked this Jesse.

They both turned and looked at Tawne, who took a step back. "Wait, you're serious? I can't drive my own car?"

"Oh, sure you can, but why would you want to? Come on and ride with me. I have wine in the back of the car and we have so much to talk about."

Tawne considered this for a moment, shrugged, then pulled her keys from her purse. She turned to Jesse. "Please, be careful. My car is all I have to my name."

"No worries, I promise to take real good care of her," Jesse said with a smile.

She handed her keys over to the hulking beast, then looked at Olivia. "I hope you'll tell me what this is all about. Dark location in the warehouse district, driver for both cars... Where exactly are we going?"

Olivia smiled and grasped Tawne's hand in hers. "I'm going to bring you to my new home. Buckle up, bestie, because I'm about to rock your fucking world!"

Tawne's eyes widened and her mouth opened, unsure what to say to this. "Who are you and what have you done with my best friend?"

Olivia giggled. "I lived my entire life having no idea..." she paused, then shook her head. "Nope, we need wine first. Come on."

Tawne nodded. "All right, but I'm still not sure about this."

"When have I ever done you wrong?"

As they approached the car, Tawne realized it wasn't just a car, but a black limo. There was another man standing beside the back passenger door. He smiled as they approached.

"Miss Martin, are we ready?" the man asked.

She nodded. "Tawne, this is Todd, our driver. Todd, this is Tawne O'Brien, my best friend since childhood."

"Miss O'Brien, it is nice to meet you."

Tawne smiled. "It's nice to meet you as well."

Todd opened the doors for them and Olivia slid in first across the leather seat. Tawne slipped inside and the door closed behind her.

The interior of the limo glowed in a soft ambience. It was almost romantic. Olivia reached for a bottle, pushed in a corkscrew and pushed a button. Seconds later, the cork was removed. She poured two glasses, handing one to Tawne.

"Cheers to our lives. May they be ever changing in the best possible way," Olivia announced.

Tawne clinked her glass. "I'll definitely drink to that."

After they sipped, Tawne sat her glass down and the limo set in motion. She noticed the windows were completely blacked out. She could not see out, and pretty sure no one could see in. She lifted a brow, then met Olivia's gaze.

"Hold onto your seat because the story I'm about to tell you will either make our friendship, or break it," Olivia told her.

She raised her brows. "Wow, okay I don't like how this has started. What's going on?"

"How do you feel about vampires and demons?"

"What? Come again?" Tawne asked.

"How do you feel about vampires and demons?"

Tawne shrugged. "I don't know what this has to do with what you have to tell me, but if I had to make a choice between them, I suppose I would say bring it on. I love reading and watching movies about vampires. Demons don't have enough stories told and like, zero movies."

Olivia smirked and sat forward in her seat. "I'm happy to hear you say that."

"Why? Did you write a book or something?"

"Or something," Olivia started, then reached across the seat, her palms up. "Give me your hands, please."

Tawne didn't hesitate. She placed her hands on top of her friend's. They held onto one another and Olivia began.

"Tawne, there's a lot about me you don't know, and it's information I was never supposed to share. *Ever.* It could have ended our friendship indefinitely."

Tawne frowned. "No one can do that."

Olivia shook her head. "These people can, and they would have. It would have resulted in your death if you knew."

"Oh shit," Tawne whispered. "Well, why are you telling me now? Have circumstances changed? Are you all right? Hell, I knew something was up when you called me! What the hell is happening?"

Olivia smiled. "It's nothing like that. Trust me, okay? I need you to remain quiet while I tell you everything. I need you to listen to me and trust what I'm telling you. Can you do that?"

Tawne nodded. Not so much that she would believe her, but more out of curiosity, now. What was so important that Olivia felt she could never trust her with this information?

"I never knew my father, which you know. My father was a demon and he was an incubus. An incubus is a male sex demon. He seduced my mother and she became pregnant with me. I was born half demon. I'm what you call a blood demon."

Tawne didn't move or flinch at that revelation.

"You're with me so far?" Olivia asked.

Tawne nodded.

"Great. All my life I was prepped for what would be called *the pairing*. It's when I come of age... Wait, let me hold off on that for a moment. There's more you need to know first." Olivia sucked a deep breath, then slowly exhaled. "Tawne, vampires are real." She paused once more.

Tawne let go of Olivia's hands and grabbed her wine. She drank the rest of it down, then reached for the bottle. She poured in the contents up to the brim, then sipped the top of her glass.

Olivia took the bottle and poured more into her own glass.

Gulping down half the glass, Tawne sat it down and turned her attention back to Olivia.

"As a blood demon," Olivia continued, "my soul purpose in life is to become a blood bag to a vampire. Moments ago, I began to say about coming of age. Well, on my last birthday, it was my time. There was a pairing ceremony put on by the vampire coven. I was brought in and dressed up as if I was going to a red-carpet gala. When I went to my pairing, there were other blood demons to be paired as well.

"Vampires who needed a blood demon, who are called concubines, came in and met each of the concubines in attendance. My vampire, Jared, accepted me first. My life has never been the same since I met him and his four brothers-at-arms."

Tawne noticed the way her eyes lit up when she mentioned Jared's name. Maybe this was who she'd been talking to in the background.

"So, in the end, I was not only paired with Jared, but his four brothers as well. I suppose you can call them my harem and I'm their queen."

Tawne took another long sip of her

wine. She put down her glass and reached for the bottle. Bringing it to her lips, she drank down some of the contents, then sat back in her seat, head relaxed back. "You're the queen of your own harem?"

"Well, that wasn't the first question I expected, but yes, I am."

Tawne felt the buzz from the wine setting in. She closed her eyes and a laugh bubbled out from her lips. The bottle of wine was removed from her grasp. She sat up and shook her head.

"So, you mean to tell me demons and vampires are real. You're a blood demon and you're mated to five vampires?"

Olivia nodded. "Precisely."

"Well, I'll be completely honest with you. This actually explains a lot about you."

Olivia's brows rose. "How do you mean?"

"You were always distant and never let

anyone in or get close to you. I mean, we were close, but I knew there was still a wall separating us. I know so much about you, but at the same time there are a lot of secrets you've kept hidden. I respected that and your privacy, but this is not what I thought it all was."

"Sometimes, Tawne, if I can be honest, there were days the depression was so bad it was like a demon sat upon my chest and I couldn't move. I didn't want to move. I wanted to lie there and give into the temptation of not living. Who would miss me if I were gone? You would. You were always there for me, always checking on me, even if I didn't need it." She sighed and lowered her gaze to the floor of the car for a moment. Giving her time to assess herself, Olivia lifted herself back up with a smile. "Now, I live a life full of love, happiness, and people who accept me for me and let me be whoever I want to be. It's amazing to have that, and quite liberating. So," she adjusted herself in her seat. "Ask me anything. You now know everything there is about me. No one else does, except for my men."

Tawne lifted a brow. "Do you have sex with them all at the same time?"

The driver, Todd, chuckled, then cleared his throat. Both women glanced his way, then Olivia chuckled.

"Yes, and no. Sometimes I am with them on a one on one basis, other times, two to three, sometimes all five at once."

"Do they bite and feed from you?"

Olivia nodded.

"Does it hurt?"

She shook her head. "Not in the least. It's actually quite erotic."

Tawne bit down on her bottom lip. "It's hard to picture you with five men at once. I mean, I don't want to see it, but I'm trying to understand how you do it."

"Do you really want to know?" Olivia

asked with a sly grin.

Tawne shook her head. "I'm good, no thanks."

Olivia sat back in her seat and laughed.

"What's so funny?" Tawne asked her.

"I've been holding that in for so long, about me being a blood demon. Only my mother knew. She knew what my life was meant for. I hated her for it for the longest time. It wasn't until recently I finally forgave her. If it weren't for her, I would never have this amazing life with my men. They truly love and adore me. They would do anything for me, be anything."

Tawne smiled and lowered her gaze. "Is that where we're going? To your home?"

"Yes. I need you in my life again, Tawne. I cannot do this without you. Call me selfish, but I think this could be a lifestyle for you as well."

"What if I were to say no?"

"Then we would return you home, no questions asked."

"Really?" Tawne asked. "But I would know everything. Wouldn't that put me at risk for exposure?"

Olivia shook her head and lowered her gaze. "No. We would wipe the memories from your mind."

"What? How?"

"It's called compulsion." Olivia sat forward in her seat. "Listen, there's still so much you don't know. In time, I truly believe you'll fall in love with part of my world. Give it a chance. You really have nothing to lose."

Tawne smiled. She'd known Olivia most of her life, but never expected to hear this news. However, it actually made a lot of sense. "I have no idea how you held onto this information your entire life and never told me. It had to eat you up inside."

Olivia nodded. "It did. There were days

I would cry myself to sleep. I was so alone in my world and only had you. Even then, I couldn't let you in."

Tawne reached across the car and pulled her friend into her arms and hugged her. "I love you so much, Olivia. Thank you for finally letting me in."

Olivia sniffed then laughed a small chuckle. "Don't thank me yet. We're having a party tonight in your honor." She pulled back enough to look into her friend's eyes. "The party is a celebration of sorts."

"What are you celebrating?"

"My anniversary with my men, and the coming inside party."

"Coming inside? What does that mean?" Tawne asked.

Olivia grinned. The car slowed and turned sharply into what felt like the bump of a driveway. "We're here. The coming inside party is for you, welcoming you into our part of the world."

Excitement peaked and Tawne's heart leapt at the thought of walking in and meeting actual vampires. "What if I said no?"

"Then I would have let you go home with no memory of tonight."

"Wow, okay then."

The car stopped, and her heart plummeted into her gut. Her feet felt heavy and she wasn't sure if she could move. The adrenaline spike quickly sobered her.

The car door opened, and the parking light turned off. Todd, the driver, stood to the side with a hand held out. "Welcome home, Miss Martin. Miss O'Brien, may I help you from the car?"

Tawne drew a deep breath and held the gaze of her best friend for a moment. Olivia nodded and motioned for her to go. She fisted her hands, then relaxed them by her legs. She could do this. She'd faced down shitty boyfriends, the loss of her parents, and being the only child with no family left. What were a few vampires and demons, right?

Tawne looked up and met Todd's gaze, then slipped her hand into his. "I'm ready."

Chapter Three

THE MIDNIGHT AIR chilled Tawne's body as she slid from the vehicle. The car door closed behind her and when she looked up, a mansion larger than she had ever seen before was laid out before her. The voice of *Robin Leach* echoed through her mind, *Lifestyles of the Rich and Famous.*

"I want to bring her to my room first to clean up," Olivia announced.

"Then we'll bring you around the back entrance to avoid foot traffic," Jesse told her.

Tawne turned and found her car parked behind the limo. Something of hers was here anyway. The lights of the limo went off and darkness consumed the area where they stood.

"Jesse, lights please?" Olivia asked.

"You got it." Jesse brought out his phone and the screen illuminated. He pressed a button and outdoor lights around the side of the home lit. "This way, ladies."

Olivia took Tawne's hand and gave it a gentle squeeze. "I live here now. My home is yours anytime you need it. You've been trusted with a great gift. My only hope is you'll accept it without judgment."

Without judgment. She would never judge Olivia for her lifestyle. When she knew her before, she'd talked often about having a ménage. Whether that was with another man or woman, it didn't matter to Olivia. She wanted to have fun, live her life the way she saw fit, damn anybody else's opinion.

Tawne smiled and squeezed her hand in return. "I won't try to pretend to understand, but you know me, I won't judge. Now, you said that you want us to clean up some?"

"Yes, and by us, I mean you." Olivia grinned and led the way toward the side entrance of the home.

When the door opened, light poured out onto the walkway. Inside were cream colored walls lined with artwork, vases— Tawne gasped. "Is that an indoor water fountain?"

Olivia smiled. "Yes, yes it is. I love that fountain."

"Holy shit," Tawne whispered. "You hit the jackpot, didn't you?"

Olivia shrugged, a sly grin playing across her lips. "Something like that."

They stepped into the hallway and the door closed behind them, Jesse on their trail.

"Jesse is my bodyguard. Whenever I leave the home, he's my detail and always with me. He's become sort of the brother I never had." She looked over her shoulder and Tawne watched her wink at the burly man. He returned the gesture with a grin.

"Aww, okay," Tawne whispered. "Other than your men, who else is here tonight?"

Olivia touched her chin and didn't answer at first.

Tawne's stomach fluttered with anticipation over what waited for her behind the closed doors. Had the vampires and demons always lived around her and she was none the wiser? How did she live in this world and never know of their existence?

She glanced at her friend and squeezed her hand once more. "I don't know how you held all this in."

Olivia smiled. "You've said that

already," she chuckled. "I promise, the understanding will settle, and soon it will be just like breathing. There's a few of the coven members here tonight. Soon, the pairing ceremony, like the one where I was paired with my men, will take place again. There's some here that are interested in alternative measures."

Tawne lifted her brow and smiled. "Alternative measures? Hmm, okay. As for the understanding, how are you so sure? You've known about this your entire life. I've been in this for five minutes."

Olivia stopped walking at the base of stairs. They were gold painted and spiraled upward. "Do you trust me?"

Tawne nodded. "Of course."

"Then let yourself go and have some fun. There are others downstairs eager to meet you. It's not often our world gets to intermingle with yours. As many questions as you may have, they'll probably have some of their own."

"Oh great. I can only imagine it will be like speed dating, but with a twist. I'll sit a table while Vampire Joe, Demon Bob, and Werewolf Tommy come over to ask me for a date."

Olivia laughed and started the ascension up the stairs. "We don't have werewolves. Sorry, I hope you're not disappointed."

"Wait," Tawne pulled her to a stop. "No shifters?"

Olivia shook her head. "Shifters, yes, werewolves like you know in the stories, no. So, we have shifters of any species you can consider, demons of all shapes and varieties, and vampires. Disappointed?"

"Hardly." They continued up the stairs and maneuvered down the hall. More portraits hung on the walls. Tawne gasped and stared up at a life size painting of her best friend. In the portrait, Olivia wore a Victorian type dress, white in color. Her dark hair hung over one shoulder while blood trickled down her neck on the other. It was tragically beautiful. "Olivia...you're so...wow!"

"One of my men is an artist. He painted me from his mind's eye like this."

"You didn't pose?"

Olivia shook her head. "He is amazing."

"I would agree with that."

Olivia took a step back and Tawne turned to follow. A few paces down, her friend opened a door to a bedroom. They walked in and Tawne gasped at the room. A king-sized four-poster bed sat against the far wall with sheer drapes hung from each column. The cream colored satin blanket and pillow were made tidy, with a few blood red and maroon throws. The walls were cream, like the part of the home she had already witnessed. A large dresser, vanity, and wardrobe set the room. It was like walking into a room for a princess.

Olivia broke the silence, "I have a dress or two I'd like you to try on. Would you mind?"

"So long as it doesn't have puffy sleeves. You might live like a princess, but we don't have to dress like one." Tawne bit her lip when Olivia raised her brow. "Oh hell, do we?"

Olivia giggled. "No, not at all. The one I have in mind for you would look amazing with your skin color and hair. It's a spaghetti strap dress, black, that's fitted to the waist. It's loose around the hips and legs with a sheer black tulle underneath."

Tawne grinned. "Well, you've sold me. Let me see it!" She looked around the room, from the vanity to the bed. "Where should I undress?"

"Wherever you like. It's just us in here.

Your bathroom is the left door over there."

Tawne followed where Olivia pointed and bit her lower lip. If the bathroom were anything like this room, she may turn into the princess from children's beast story and never leave her room. She removed her clothes and laid them across the bed. "What shoes will I wear?"

"There's a few we can try. Go for comfort over style. Trust me on this. You'll be standing a lot."

"Right," she said and sat down on the edge of the bed. The comforter chilled her backside and she ran her hands over the fabric. It was softer than any blanket or bedspread she had ever laid her hands on.

Mesmerized with the room, Tawne didn't realize Olivia had disappeared through the other doorway until she reappeared.

"Here we are," Olivia said and brought

out a black dress from what had to be the closet. "I think this will be perfect on you." She unzipped the backside and held it down.

Tawne stood and grabbed one of the bedposts, then stepped gingerly into the dress. Olivia brought it up over her hips to her upper body and she slipped her arms through the slender straps, then turned around. "Oh, your hands are cold!"

Olivia chuckled and zipped up the dress. "Sorry about that. Turn and let me see you."

Tawne turned around to face her and placed her hands on her hips. "Oh, Olivia, this dress, it's everything! I feel... Hell, you're going to make me say it, aren't you?"

She laughed and nodded. "Yes, I am. Say it."

"I feel like a damn princess!" Tawne laughed and shook her head. "What shoes, and is there makeup in the vanity?"

Olivia pointed toward the dressing table. "Yes, help yourself. I'm going to figure out the shoes."

Tawne opened one of the drawers to the dressing table and smiled at the contents inside. Organized the only way Olivia would have it, the eye shadows, blushes, and eye pencils were set inside. She pulled out a few pallets, then opened the next drawer. Inside were foundations, powers, and mascara. She picked the colors to match her skin tone and began to apply the makeup. Moments later, she applied the mascara. The top drawer on the other side held lipstick and lip-gloss. She picked up a soft pink lipstick and applied it to her lips. She smiled and stood from the vanity.

"You need earrings and a necklace to go with these shoes."

Tawne turned to find Olivia leaning

against the bedpost. She had managed to change into a red, fitted dress and black heels. Tawne gasped at what she held in her hands. "Are those—"

"Yes," Olivia giggled.

They were close-toed, low heels and across the top sat a glittering butterfly. She hoped it was glass and not diamonds, but the hell with it. She would feel like Cinderella tonight.

Olivia handed over the shoes and Tawne held them like they were precious gems. "I don't know if I can wear these," Tawne whispered.

"Why not? They're only shoes."

"They're not just shoes, they're *Louboutin!*"

"And they're mine on loan to you. So, you can definitely wear them." Olivia reached around her and opened a jewelry box. A song played from it and glancing over at it, Tawne wondered if she would see a small ballerina dancing. Sure enough, a white swan dancer spun in circles. "This box was mine when I was a child."

"I recognize it," Tawne whispered. "I still can't believe this is happening."

Olivia smiled and picked up a pair of diamond earrings, then a silver chain with a tear drop diamond. "Here, put these on. It'll be perfect."

"I don't understand the fuss for all of this. It's a dinner party, right?"

Olivia nodded. "And you're the guest of honor. Everyone is dressed up for the occasion. It's not quite a black tie, formal ball, but something like that."

"Oh," Tawne whispered. "But why? Why for me?"

"I already told you. You're new to our world and it's a historic event," Olivia said with a smile.

Tawne nodded and put on the earrings then the necklace. She slipped on the shoes and stood.

Olivia smiled and pressed her hands together. "You look exquisite!"

"Thank you. I feel exquisite. I don't know when you managed to change so quickly, but you look hot!"

Olivia giggled. "Why, thank you. Are you ready for your introduction?"

Her throat suddenly felt dry. "Can I have a shot of something before we head down?"

Her best friend smirked. "It's best if you don't. I wouldn't want you stumbling down the stairs. You'll be fine. I'll be there the entire time."

Tawne nodded then walked out of the room. She held onto Olivia's hand and squeezed it. "How do I act? What do I say? What do I do if someone wants to feed from me?" The questions rushed from her before she had a chance to think about what she wanted to ask.

Olivia grinned. "Just be yourself and everything else will fall into place. No one will feed from you without your permission. Trust me, though, nothing like that will happen to you tonight."

Tawne nodded, and they made it as far as the staircase before Olivia turned to her and placed her hands on Tawne's arms.

"You've got this. One step at a time. I'll see you at the bottom."

"Wait, you're not walking with me?"

Olivia smiled. "No, you're a princess now, remember?"

Tawne stuck out her tongue, then grinned. "Go on. Pray for me I won't slip."

Olivia took the stairs down and Tawne watched her descend in the spiral rotation. She hadn't realized music was playing. It wasn't until it stopped and a semi-silence descended over her that she realized it had been. The murmuring of voices from below ceased, and she could barely hear her friend announce her arrival.

Her heart sped in her chest and if she wasn't careful, it would leap free and run away, leaving her body behind. She gripped the stair rail and began her decent, one step at a time. The staircase twined downward and the bottom floor appeared.

Dark pants and black shoes came into view, followed by dress jackets of suits and tuxedos. The men turned toward the staircase and Tawne's breath caught in her throat. Every one of the men stared up at her and each of them were the most attractive specimen of males she had ever laid her eyes on.

She heard Olivia clear her throat and it was then she realized she had stopped on the stairs. A heat rushed over her neck and up her cheeks. She smiled, hoping to cover the moment of embarrassment before starting forward once again. Once at the bottom, she made her way over the polished floor to

Olivia.

"You must be Tawne," asked a man who came up behind her best friend. He placed his hands possessively on Olivia's shoulders. "My name is Jared. Welcome to our home. It's a pleasure to meet you."

Tawne's brows rose. This was one of her men? Holy hell, he was gorgeous.

"Yes, this is Tawne," Olivia answered with a grin. "Tawne, this is my Jared."

"Hi-Hi," Tawne started and cleared her throat. "Very nice to meet you."

"*Mia Bella*," came two more men. "Is this your beloved Tawne?"

Tawne's mouth opened slightly. The man who spoke had shoulder length dark hair with soft curls. A man who looked similar to Jared stood beside him.

"Yes, my love," Olivia answered. "Tawne, this is Landon," she motioned to the one with the curls. "And this is Jake, Jared's brother." Both men held their hands out for her.

She accepted Jake's first as he stood closer to her. "Nice to meet you."

She turned to Landon. He took her hand and pulled it to his lips. He feathered his lips over the back of her hand, then let her go. "The pleasure is mine."

"Oh," she whispered and felt a heat rise in her body once more. How did Olivia deal with these men?

"Ah, this must be the beautiful Tawne."

She turned to a man with skin like smooth, dark chocolate who approached. She smiled and nodded.

"Well, allow me to introduce myself. I'm Aidan and it's very nice to finally meet you."

She sighed a long breath and met her friend's gaze.

"We'll leave you to it," Jared whispered and pressed his lips against Olivia's cheek."

She smiled and each of her men walked their separate ways.

Tawne shook her head. "I'm not going to even pretend to understand any of this."

"There's nothing to understand," Olivia told her. "It feels like they were made for me, and me for them. I can't imagine my life without them in it. We are bonded in a way I am still trying to understand." She waved off that last comment. "I'm getting ahead of myself. Come, there's others here looking forward to meeting you."

Tawne grasped Olivia's outstretched hand and allowed herself to be escorted into the main part of the room. Men and women stood, talking amongst themselves. One by one, each person turned to face her, and she wondered who were the vampires and who were the demons. Considering everyone appeared to be human, she decided to not try too hard in deciphering anything right now. Instead, she decided to go with the flow. She would follow Olivia's lead and if anything, she would hide out at the bar and people watch.

Then, as if the crowd parted, like Moses split the red seas, four men walked into the room and Tawne's breath caught in her throat. She squeezed Olivia's hand and heard her friend hiss.

"Ow, Tawne. What's wrong?"

"Who in the hell is that?" she whispered.

Olivia turned around, then smiled. She looked back at Tawne with a smirk filled with mischief. "Would you like to meet them?"

Tawne's stomach flirted with intense desire in wanting to know who these men were. She loosened the tight grip on her friend's hand, then nodded. "Yes, please. I feel as if I have been asleep for years and only just now woke."

Olivia grinned a little wider. "Get ready to be swept off your feet by a passion you've only read about."

Chapter Four

THEY SAY MAN was made in the image of God, but the vampires who stood before Tawne were sculpted from a different sort of clay. The Greek Gods she read about in school had nothing on the men in the room. Long hair tied to the nape of a strong neck, or short cut business with a slight beard growth. Most were tall, and all were breathtaking. She was a kid in the candy store, but the candies in this scenario were the men, and she was ready to shop until she'd satiated her sweet tooth.

"How do you do it?" Tawne whispered to Olivia. "Seriously, how?"

Olivia grinned. "We just let it happen. We'll talk details later. First, we need to get you properly introduced to our guests."

Tawne nibbled on her bottom lip. They walked further into the center of the room. Men and women were mingling, carrying on conversations about who knows what. In the past, most parties she'd attended she was either with Olivia or another friend. They people watched and kept their distance from either the rough guy or the crazy party girl.

However, here, in this setting, Tawne wasn't sure who may be who in this scenario.

Do vampires get drunk?

Do they eat or drink anything other than blood?

What happens if they feed on her?

Would she survive the bite or be turned into a vampire?

So many questions, but it wasn't the time or place...at least, not yet.

"Our coven frowns upon humans knowing of our existence," Olivia told her. "No coven members are here tonight, but they'll find out soon enough about you."

Tawne frowned. "What does that mean for me?"

"Nothing, right now. They're not going to make you do anything you don't want to do or are not comfortable with. We'll discuss this later as well."

"What happens if one of them bites me?"

Olivia chuckled. "No one will ever do that to you without your consent."

Tawne noticed Olivia's face lose some of its luster with the comment she'd made. Making a mental note to bring this up later, she looked down at her hands.

Fidgeting with her fingers, she whispered, "I don't know what to say or do."

Across the room, Tawne spied a man in a gray business suit. His back to her, she felt free to ogle his wide shoulders and thick arms. The arms of his jacket clung to what could only be muscles Tawne imagined. Her gaze drifted down his body and she lifted a brow at the roundness of his ass. She pictured herself on her back, reaching around this man's body, grabbing a handful of his delectable backside.

The man turned, and his gaze met hers. He smirked and winked at her.

Feeling a blush rush to her cheeks, she lowered her gaze and grabbed Olivia's hand. Yanking her friend toward her, she whispered, "Please, tell me they cannot my read mind. For all things holy, please, tell me they can't."

A soft laugh escaped Olivia and she

carefully removed the grip Tawne held on her hand. "No, they can't read minds."

"Oh, thank gawd," she sighed.

"However…"

"Oh shit," Tawne whispered and cringed to think what information Olivia may be about to deliver.

"They can sense a change in the air. Kind of like the weather. It's cool but if the sun were to come out and warm up the atmosphere, they would feel that, but within us."

"Oh, so if I were casual then got caught up checking out a delicious ass on a man, and it made my mood change, he would pick up on that?"

Olivia nodded. "Exactly."

"Well, hell, he might as well read minds then!"

Giggling, Olivia took a side step then let go of Tawne. "Tawne, allow me to introduce to you Cristofano Moretti. He's a financial advisor to his family and the coven. He loves cars and motorcycles. Cris," she turned to the man who joined the two of them. "This is my very best friend, Tawne. She's from my hometown of New Orleans. Tawne's family is from Ireland and she's a full-time student, learning about history. She has a goal to become a museum curator."

Tawne stared at the man before her. Tall, dark, with an ass like a snack, he smiled down at her. His hair was longish on top, cut short on the sides, and styled up in a modern look men wore. His hair was like the color of an Autumn morning with a small gray line of hair in the front. His face had a close cut beard. She wanted to run her hands through his hair and feel his face between her legs.

What the hell is wrong with me?

"Very nice to meet you," Cristofano said and held his hand out.

She placed her hand in his and her lips parted. A squeak slipped from between her lips when he lifted her hand and fleetingly pressed his lips to the back of her wrist. "H-H-Hi..."

"Please, call me Cris."

She blinked. Momentarily breathless as she battled to control the heat rushing within her over that single, simple caress of his mouth over her hand, she startled and sucked a deep breath.

Get control of yourself, woman!

She blurted out, "I've never ridden a motorcycle."

Cristofano lifted his brows, then grinned. "Then maybe one evening I may escort you on a ride."

She noticed an accent when he spoke. One that sent a delicious chill skating down her spine. She nodded. "I would like that. May I ask, where are you from?"

"Originally from Venice, Italy. I have been here for many years, though. Louisiana is now my home."

She smiled. "I've never been outside the US. I'd love to travel one day."

He grinned. "Maybe one day you will. Until then, may I get you a drink?" He lifted a crimson substance to his lips that appeared thick. It didn't congeal, but was it blood?

She swallowed a hard lump, then nodded. "I like merlot."

"Then I'll bring you a merlot. Olivia," he nodded to her friend.

"Cris."

As Cristofano walked away, Tawne found herself watching him with a grin. "Oh my goodness, Olivia. Cristofano from Venice... I could eat him alive."

"Wait until you meet his brothers," Olivia whispered to her.

"What?" Alarm set in and she shook her head. "No, I can't... I couldn't possibly do what you do."

"What I do?" Olivia asked. "Listen, there's a lot to talk about later, and I promise we will, but just because he has brothers means nothing about nothing. Meet and mingle. Let things progress. Don't be so hard to judge at first glance. Everyone here, except for the blood demons like me, were once human. Take that into consideration. Most people here had no choice in becoming what they are. You, however, are different."

Tawne looked at the floor. She pictured the woman from *Game of Thrones* who repeated Shame, Shame, Shame over and over while ringing a bell. "I'm so sorry," she whispered. "I didn't mean to be rude. I promise. It's just so much to take in."

"One at a time, okay?"

She nodded and let out a long sigh. "I've got this. Who's next?"

Olivia grinned. "That's my girl. Now, come on, I'll introduce you to his brothers."

"Do vampires normally form a family

like this?"

Olivia looked at her friend. "You could say that. When I met my men, I thought only Jared claimed me. It wasn't until I found out about his brothers I realized it was a package deal."

"Is it a hard life to juggle, having five men?"

Olivia shook her head. "Not at all. I never thought I could love five men at the same time, but here I am doing it."

Tawne nodded. "I believe you, and Olivia, you look so unbelievably happy."

Her friend smiled. "That's because I am. Now," she paused and turned toward a group of men, then casually pointed toward a man. He was tall like Cristofano, but his hair was jet black and cut short. He chuckled and turned slightly when he took a drink. Where Cristofano's skin was olive in tone, his was paler. Dark facial scruff covered his cheeks and his full lips captured the glass between them. Then he glanced at Tawne from the corner of his eyes.

He lowered his glass and said something to the group of men he was chatting with, then turned to face her. Their eyes met and Tawne gasped. His eyes were beautiful, like the morning ocean after a storm. She felt her body shiver with anticipation of this man looking directly into her soul.

As he crossed the room toward them, he smiled and held out his hand. "You must be new here."

She grasped his hand and nodded. Like before, she opened her mouth, but nothing came out.

Olivia cleared her throat. "Tawne, allow me to introduce you to Will. He's an attorney and works for the same practice as my Ethan. Will, this is my best friend Tawne."

Will, like Cristofano, pressed his lips to the back of her hand, then let her go.

"Pleasure to meet you. You're human?"

The question almost came off as a sneer. She let it go, like Olivia told her, not to judge. She nodded. "Yes, that's right. What law do you practice?"

He shrugged. "Depends, but mainly contracts."

"Oh, is that interesting?"

"Not really," he told her and took a step back. "I need to grab another drink. Are you staying here with Olivia?"

She nodded. "Yes, I am."

"Well, then I guess I'll be seeing you around." He glanced at Olivia. "Olivia," then turned away.

Tawne lifted her brow and looked at her friend. "Was it me, or was he a little curt?"

Olivia sighed and nodded. "Yeah, that's Will. He comes off as cold, but get through that tough exterior, you have a knight in shining armor."

"Is it tarnished?"

Olivia smirked. "All the best knights have tarnished armor."

Tawne grinned. "He was so hot. The bad boy thing kind of makes him a little hotter."

Grinning, Olivia winked at her. "Then keep it in mind. Evan," she called out.

Tawne shifted her gaze from the retreating back of Will to the man who approached. His hair was similar to how Cristofano styled his, but it was darker. He smiled as he drew near. Dark suit and red tie, blue eyes and white teeth. Like the two others before, he was right off a magazine cover exquisite.

"Tawne," Olivia started with her introduction, "this is Evan Wilson. Evan is from New York originally and is an accountant. He does work for Ethan's firm and the coven. Evan, this is my best friend Tawne."

"My oh my, my sweet cherry pie." Evan waggled his brows and held his hand out for hers. Tawne took it and he lifted it up, brushing his mouth over the back of her hand. "How have you found yourself this evening, Miss Tawne? You are as beautiful as your name."

She grinned and felt the blood rush to her cheeks and warm her in a delightful way. "You're a charmer, aren't you?"

He chuckled. "I like having a good time as much as any man."

"Your drink, my lady," Cristofano interrupted and handed her a glass. He turned to face Evan. "I see you've met the beautiful, Tawne."

"Yes, brother, I sure have. Isn't she pure perfection?"

"Indeed, I agree," Cristofano answered. "Don't let him sweep you off your feet too soon." He leaned into her ear and whispered, "Allow all of us to do that for you."

She grinned and met Cristofano's gaze. "I'll see what I can do."

Evan chuckled. "You're the most beautiful thing in this room, pardon Miss Olivia, of course."

"No offense," Olivia grinned. "I would like to introduce her to Chayton."

"I'll get him for you," Cristofano turned. "He was at the pool table last I saw him."

"Nice to meet you, Miss Tawne." Evan stepped closer and placed a gentle finger under her chin. "I look forward to seeing you again, very soon." He leaned in.

Tawne's heart skipped to a quicker beat when his lips met her skin.

She struggled to open her mouth to say something back when, "Me, too," stumbled out.

He grinned and met her gaze. "Your hair is like a fire that has been extinguished for so long. Your eyes are a beautiful green of the forest. You are a vision."

"I could listen to you all day, but I'm

afraid I would become shallow with all the compliments."

He chuckled. "Then, I would have to make sure to keep you grounded."

Oh yes, Tawne was in heaven here with the vampires. All the stories she read, the movies she watched, did nothing for what stood before her.

Evan looked past her and nodded. "Here comes our brother, Chayton."

She turned her back to Evan. Approaching was a man whose skin was tan like a delicious color of butterscotch. His onyx hair was long, past his shoulders. He appeared to be Native American. The man, like his brothers, was breathtaking.

He smiled and held out his hand. "Hi there, I'm Chayton Blair."

She took his hand. "Hello, I'm Tawne."

"Tawne," he placed his other hand on top of hers and took a step closer. "Welcome to our small part of the world.

It is truly a pleasure meeting you."

She smiled. "Thank you."

"Chayton, tell her a little about what you're working on," Olivia asked and took a step back from the duo.

"Absolutely." He continued to hold onto her hand when he began. "I'm a doctor. I do research for the coven and looking to perfect a serum I'm working on."

"Sounds exciting," she told him. "What is the serum for?"

"It is a way to make synthetic blood for us."

She raised a brow. "How do you mean?"

Chayton glanced at Olivia and she nodded. "Go ahead. She knows of me being a blood demon."

He nodded and shifted his attention back to Tawne. "Vampires can only survive on the blood of a blood demon, like your friend here."

Tawne nodded. "Right, that's what Olivia told me. You're creating a way to survive without needing the blood of a demon?"

"Exactly. My hope is to make it successful in the coming weeks. I'm oh-so-close!"

She smiled at his excitement. "And here I am studying history when there's a whole new world I've never known anything about."

He leaned in. "Our possibilities are endless!"

She giggled and pulled her hand free from his. Sipping her merlot, she found Cristofano returning to the room with Evan and Will just behind him. She thought of the four men courting her all at the same time. How would she do it? Well, would they actually want to see her? How does this dating work between humans and vampires? Was it even allowed?

"I'll be right back. I'm leaving you in very capable hands," Olivia told her. "Now, Chayton, protect my friend. Don't let any danger come to her or you'll answer to me."

Chayton grinned, then chuckled. "I promise to protect her with my life, my lady!"

Tawne laughed and covered her lips with her hand. Moments later, Cristofano, Will, and Evan joined Chayton.

"It truly has been a pleasure to meet you this evening," Cristofano announced. "Would you consider visiting us at our home?"

She met the gaze of three of the four men. Will had his eyes lowered to the ground but didn't say anything.

"Yes, I would be happy to, so long as I'm welcomed by all."

Will lifted his eyes and met her gaze. Neither said anything, just stared. Will lifted his brow, then looked at Cristofano. "Do what you want. You know where you'll find me." He then turned to leave.

"Ignore him," Chayton told her. "He welcomes you as well."

She smiled. "I'm sure he just takes some warming up to."

"Something like that," Evan added.

Cristofano took her hands in his. "We'll set up the trip with Jared and Jesse. Once a plan is in place, we'll have you escorted over."

She nodded. "I'm looking forward to it."

He leaned in, then hesitated. "May I kiss your cheek?"

She smiled. "Yes, you may."

Cristofano cupped her cheeks and tilted her head up. He leaned in and feathered a kiss just on the corner of her mouth. "I can hardly stand the wait."

Her knees weakened, and her panties grew wet with need. She nibbled on her bottom lip and smiled.

A hand caressed the back of her neck and when she looked over, it was Chayton. "*Winyan*, you are beautiful, and if I may be so bold to admit, hard to resist."

She turned to face Chayton as Cristofano released her. "What does *Winyan* mean?"

"Woman, in Sioux. My name, Chayton, means Falcon." He leaned in and, like Cristofano, swept his lips over her cheek.

"She will be spoiled by us and never want to return home," Evan told them.

She met his gaze and when he smiled, she could see his fangs. A part of her had thought this would scare her, or maybe remind her they're the predator where she's the prey. In this moment, though, surrounded by these men, she never felt safer.

"Enjoy the rest of your evening," Cristofano told her. "You have made this wonderful night unforgettable."

The three men left her side and she stood momentarily alone. She pressed her lips together and when she turned, Olivia was behind her, smiling like a damned Cheshire Cat.

"I told you," Olivia whispered. "Are you ready for this part of my world?"

"I have never been more ready for anything in my life!" Tawne's heart leapt and excitement pulsed through her veins. Then she thought of Will and her smile drooped slightly. "Except for Will. He doesn't seem to care for me very much."

"Give him time," Olivia took her hands and pulled her toward the bar. "Think of him like a wounded dog. He just needs some time. I promise, he'll come around."

Tawne nodded and slid onto a leather topped seat at the bar. She lifted her gaze to the back wall. Bottles of liquor lined the mirrored wall. She watched her own reflection, then just behind her, off to the side, tucked into a dark corner, stood

Will. And his eyes were hard on hers.

She lifted one side of her mouth in a half smile, then lowered her gaze. Maybe playing coy was what she needed to do. When she looked up again, Will had left. She picked up her merlot, savored a long sip, and thought about the men she'd met, and the family that had become Olivia's. Would this be her fate, if she accepted it?

Chapter Five

YESTERDAY, TAWNE WOKE as a human with the love of a good book, preferably vampire novels. She longed for the darkness, for someone to be as passionate with her as she read in the pages of her books. She needed a love like this to seduce and claim her as their own.

Today, she woke as a brand new woman where the fantasy could become her reality. A grin spread from corner to corner of her lips and a squeal interrupted the silence of her bedroom.

The cream bedspread chilled her skin upon the touch. She sat up and scooted back to the headboard and pulled her legs to her chest. She stared across the room the vanity setup, her reflection in the mirror showing her disheveled hair.

Cristofano, the money man, the investor, the patient one...or so he appeared. He had an air of leadership about him as well. His eyes could stare into her soul and read her mind, body, and soul. The way he leaned in and pressed the kiss on her cheek, she'd felt like *Scarlett O'Hara* in the arms of *Rhett Butler*. No one had ever whispered such words of lust. Her body shivered with the delicious thoughts of seduction.

Then there was Chayton, the doctor, the sexy-as-sin vampire who swooped in and captured a kiss, like Cristofano did, without warning. His hands were gentle yet held her with need. He could possess her body with a touch of his finger and she would yield to him on bended knee, bound any way he would take her.

I've never been tied up or dominated before. I wonder what it would be like? Feel like? Multiplied by four?

Her smile was replaced by a mischievous smirk as Evan came to her mind next. The accountant, the numbers man. There was a mysterious side to him that she wanted to discover. Each man would have a story to tell. What would be his? Espionage? The stories a spy could tell sent excitement racing through her.

She imagined the books she read in the past where the hero was an undercover operative. No, that wouldn't be Evan. If there was a spy in the group, if there was someone willing to hide everything from everyone, it would be Will. He had this hard exterior, like a solid wall of concrete standing up against the fiercest of storms. No cracks, no breakage, no getting in unless he opened the door and allowed entrance. It was up to Tawne to gain his trust and earn acceptance into his world. If he was part of the package deal, she may have her work cut out for her. She was never one to chase a man, but, with Will, she would consider letting her own defenses down to allow her to get to know him better. Something happened that made him this way, but what? Time would definitely tell.

She pulled the covers back and slid to the edge of the bed. A chill raced up her legs from the coldness of the floor on her bare feet. She needed to see Olivia soon, but first, bathroom and a shower.

***

Standing in front of her mirror, Tawne had never been more scared of anything in her life. She was in a foreign house, with foreign people, and a woman who was her best friend. Although, now it felt as if she barely knew Olivia. The woman she'd known her entire life was a blood demon. What did this mean for Olivia?

She was basically a living blood bag to her vampires.

Her vampires, all five of them, loved and adored her in a way Tawne had not witnessed or heard of. Was it possible to love more than one person at a time? Possibly, but how did the men not grow jealous of one another?

She shook her head and inhaled a long, deep breath, then let it go with a soft raspberry blowing between her lips. She came here to learn, to understand, to take a new adventure. She laughed to herself.

Adventure definitely. Fearful? A little. Exciting? Hell yes.

She took a few steps toward the bedroom door, then wondered what time it was.

Was it morning? Afternoon?

Did the vampires move around during the day or did they sleep?

Do they sleep?

Do they drink human blood as well as demon?

She grasped the doorknob and turned it. The door clicked and opened slightly. Cool air seeped through, sending another chill brushing down her spine and goose bumps to pebble over her arms. What would be on the other side? Potentially her future, but right now, she would settle for a blank wall.

Closing her eyes, she grasped the knob, quickly opened the door and stepped through before she could lose her nerve.

"What are you doing?"

She gasped and opened her eyes. Will stood before her with a frown. He wore a tight fitting, black t-shirt with a gray painted eagle brand on it, denim jeans, and black boots.

Her mouth opened, and a squeak came out.

He lifted a brow, then rolled his eyes. "Right," he mumbled and sidestepped her. "You're standing blind in the hallway and taking up walking space. If you're going to insist on closing your eyes like a child, maybe retreat to your room and play." He continued to belittle her. "It's not often one walks from their room blind, especially not knowing the layout of the house."

Embarrassment filled her and she felt blood rush to her cheeks. His shoulder brushed against hers ever so softly. First he humiliated her, then he purposely bumped into her. Anger rose, and her hands fisted at her sides. She wanted to turn and give Will a piece of her mind. Why was he being so arrogant toward her? What the hell did she do to him? They'd just met.

As she began to turn, a whisper

sounded just next to her ear. A pair of hands cradled the back of her head. Thumbs pressed into the nape of her neck and he tilted her head to the side. "One could break their neck on the stairs, if one is not careful."

A breath shuddered from her lips and she leaned her head back against Will. "Would you allow me to fall?"

"Yeah, I would," he growled and released her.

Tawne stumbled backward and turned to catch her balance. She stared down the hall, but Will was nowhere in sight. Did he put her down, tease her, then run off before she could say anything? It sure looked that way.

Talk about being a confusing asshole. I hate you, but I want to seduce you, just so you can fall on your ass.

She groaned and made her way to the end of the hall to the spiral staircase. She descended and followed the smell of food cooking. Her shoes struck the marble floor and the closer she came to food, the further her anger fled.

Will can go fuck himself. I need to eat, then I'll consider what I may say—or do— to him.

She turned the corner and found the kitchen, and inside it was Jake, one of Olivia's men. He either heard her come into the kitchen or heard the sound of her belly grumble.

"Good afternoon, Tawne. Have a seat," he offered.

She smiled. "Thank you. At least someone is being pleasant to me this morning—wait, you said afternoon?"

He chuckled. "That I did. It's around two, maybe three? I'm not sure. Time doesn't matter much when you're immortal."

"Yeah, I suppose so. May I ask what you're making?"

He nodded. "Chicken Florentine. I

knew you would be hungry, and this is one of Olivia's favorite meals."

Tawne smiled. "That's nice to hear."

"Now," he set a plate with food on it in front of her. "Tell me about what happened with Will?"

She blinked, then raised a brow. "How did you know?"

He smirked. "He's an asshole to everyone."

"Oh, well, I suppose that makes me feel a little better." She took a bite, then groaned as the flavor exploded in her mouth. "Holy shit, you should be a chef!"

He chuckled. "Thank you." He crossed his arms over his body and leaned against the counter. "So, what are your thoughts so far being in our world?"

She chewed on another bite, then swallowed. "I'm not sure yet, but to be honest, finding this out, and about Olivia, it makes a lot of sense."

"How's that?"

"Yeah, how's that?"

They both turned to Olivia entering the room. She wore a beautiful, light pink halter sundress with white wedge sandals. Her hair was braided over her shoulder with soft loose curls falling in tendrils around her cheeks.

Tawne smiled and took another bite. Once she swallowed, she answered. "You were mysterious about so many things, like I told you. There was so much I didn't know, but when you filled me in, it just kinda made sense. I'm not sure how to explain it. As for this world," she looked at Jake. "I think I'm going to really enjoy it. There's a whole new world to explore, learn about, and take in. It's my thing, you know, learning and absorbing."

Olivia stepped toward Jake and the two embraced. He feathered his mouth over her lips and trailed a finger across her cheek.

"You look beautiful, my love," he whispered.

Tawne felt like she was spying on a private moment between two lovers. She lowered her gaze to her plate and stared at the half-eaten food.

"How do you do it?" The question left her before she could recall it. She lifted her gaze to Olivia, then to Jake.

"How do we do what?" Olivia asked.

Tawne gave a quick smile. "I'm trying to understand how you can be with five men at once and love them all. I'm also trying to understand how all five of you don't get jealous or fight over her."

"Let me see if I can answer this," Jake offered.

Olivia smiled and removed her arms from around his waist.

He stepped over to the bar table and leaned against it. "We are brothers. We are five, but we are also as one. We knew many years ago we were destined for one woman to be shared between the five of us. We knew we would find the one woman who could tame, love, and handle all of us at once. It takes a special person to open her heart wide enough for five souls. The moment Olivia stepped into the claiming ceremony, we knew, right then, she was the one. Her scent, her smile, everything about her told us she was the missing piece to our puzzle. Because of Olivia, we are now complete."

"That's beautiful, Jake, thank you," Olivia whispered.

"I meant every word."

Tawne watched the bond between her best friend and one of her five men. There was a strength between them she'd never known. She had never experienced it, and she longed for it more than anything.

She took her last few bites and stood from the bar. "Thank you. I appreciate the honesty. I can tell you truly love her, and she loves you." Tawne shook her head and handed her plate to Jake when he reached for it. "Thank you," she whispered. "I have a lot to learn, it seems."

"No, you don't," Olivia told her. "Don't think. Just be."

"Just be?"

"Yes." Her best friend walked around the counter. She took Tawne's hands and squeezed them. "Stop thinking. Let your heart lead you. You'll figure it out. I promise. Cris, Evan, and Chayton...they're very interested in pursuing you."

"And Will?"

"He'll come around," Jake answered. "Trust me. He's a dick, but once you're through the iron exterior, he's all soft and shit inside."

"Soft and shit?" Tawne repeated with a chuckle. "I'll take your word on it. I suppose time will tell."

Olivia nodded. "Give it time. Meanwhile, the men would like to share their home with you. It's perfectly safe and not too far from where we are. It'll allow you to get to know them on a deeper level, and see if this is a world you would like to live in."

"Go and stay with them?" Tawne asked. "Leave here and move in with them?"

"Well, when you put it that way, yeah, that sounds weird, but it's what happened with me. After my claiming, I came home with my men. We worked our way up to where we are now. It took a lot of trust on my part. They also respected me, my decisions, and never pushed me into anything. I expect it'll be the same with your men."

Tawne grinned. "*My* men? No, they're not my men. I would love for them to be my men, but they're not. I'm not a blood demon, like you. How can they sustain their life with me being a human? How would they eat?"

Olivia smiled once more. "I'm telling you, give it time. Please, trust me. Everything will work out if you give it a chance."

Tawne nodded. "Okay, fine. I'll play it your way." She released her friend's hands and glanced back at Jake. "Thank you again for the late lunch, early dinner? It was amazing."

"Anytime."

As she was leaving the kitchen, hushed whispers and giggles interrupted the deafening silence that rang in Tawne's ears. As far back as she could remember, she wanted a love so fierce, so strong, it would knock her on her ass and make her second guess everything that had ever happened in her life. She wanted exactly what Olivia had, and now it was up to her to woman up and go out there and claim it. If she were destined to be the concubine for the quartet of vampires that had been thrust into her life, then she would do what was required to make that happen. Love was not instant, and she knew this. She also wasn't against spending her time with the four breathtaking vampires to see where it may lead them. Sometimes finding love involved taking a leap of immense proportions. In this case, it was a vault for her life off a monumental bridge with a bottomless universe. She had never felt fear like this, and she embraced the challenge.

Chapter Six

TAWNE STARED AT Jesse, the bodyguard who had been hired to protect Olivia in her men's absence. His large frame towered over hers and she felt her mouth run dry.

"Arrangements have been made for your belongings to be delivered as soon as possible."

She blinked but couldn't speak. She gave herself the pep talk of grabbing the theoretical bull by the make believe horns, yet when the opportunity arose for her to take the first step, she froze.

"Miss Tawne, did you understand me?" Jesse asked.

She still didn't speak.

Four vampires.

One human.

Four sexy, drool-worthy vampires.

Me. A human.

Four sinfully delicious, fuck-worthy, longing to be tasted and seduced vampires.

And me, the human ready to dive in head first.

She smiled, then offered a nod. "Yes, understood. I, umm—"

"Don't worry about it. You should've seen Olivia during her pairing ceremony. She was completely against all of it."

She raised her brows. "Really? What changed then?"

"Meeting her match. Well, matches in this case. I'm going to tell you what I told her. Take it one day, and one step at a time. No one will make you do anything you're not comfortable with. You can stop this at any time. Just understand what comes with leaving."

She nodded. "My mind will be wiped clean of all of this."

"That's right."

"Jesse, may I ask you a personal question?"

"Shoot." He crossed his thick arms over his chest and his brows furrowed as if he were concentrating. Jesse was someone she would not want to meet in a dark alley.

"How are you able to do this, as a human? Don't you get lonely not having a woman of your own?" She paused, then looked at the floor. "I hope I'm not overstepping."

He chuckled. Tawne looked back up at him and met his gaze. "It's fine to ask. But what makes you think I'm human?"

Her browse rose in surprise. "You're

not human?"

"I never said I was or wasn't. You're assuming I am."

She frowned. "You're confusing me, Jesse. Are you human or demon or something else?"

He winked at her. "Didn't mean to confuse, but what difference does it make if I'm human or not?"

She shrugged. "End of the day, it doesn't matter to anyone, I suppose. I was curious, with me being human and knowing the secrets of this world, and how it worked with you."

"I've been with the coven for a long time. That's all you need to know."

She nodded. "Fair enough. What should I expect when I get there?"

"Well, they're opening their home for you as a guest. Enjoy your time there with them and see what it brings you. There have been humans involved with vampires in the past. It's not unheard of... I can tell you're wondering."

"I figured as much with humans and vampires. I mean, it's in so many love stories."

He leaned in with a smirk. "They've never written vampires like the ones that live here, though." Jesse winked again.

She grinned and shook her head. "Jesse, I think we're going to be really good friends."

He chuckled once more and stepped past her. "The car will be waiting for you outside. The guys know you're coming and from what I was told, are looking forward to having you there."

"I'm sure not all of them," she mumbled.

"You might be surprised what you find out about all of them," he told her as he left the room.

Tawne turned back to the room she'd stayed in the last few nights. Hearing a meow at the door, she turned and found

Sherlock, Olivia's cat. She bent down and Sherlock came up to her, bumping his head against her hand.

"Well, it's nice to see you again. Are you enjoying your new home?"

Something caught his attention and Sherlock meowed, then ran back out of the room.

She sighed and stood, then turned toward her bed. Her suitcase was packed, and her stomach flipped with nerves. She couldn't tell if she was excited, or about to vomit.

"Are you ready?"

Hearing Olivia, Tawne turned to the door and smiled at her friend holding her cat.

"Sherlock was just in here with me. I guess he heard you coming?"

Olivia nodded. "Probably."

"Yeah, I think I'm ready, but Olivia?"

"Yeah?" She sat down on the bed and placed her cat next to her.

"I've never done anything like this before."

Olivia smiled and reached for Tawne's hand. "I hadn't either when I stepped into my pairing ceremony. It would have been thrust upon me whether I wanted it or not, so I accepted it and here we are."

"You were scared, though, right?"

"Totally wanted to crap myself the night of my pairing. Imagine the first night spent in my new home!"

Tawne shook her head. "I wish I had known back then. I'm still so sorry you had to carry this on your shoulders for all those years."

Olivia smiled. "Don't worry about any of that. It was my burden to carry. Besides, we went through quite a few meetings with the coven to get this pass for you."

"The coven? That's like your vampire counsel, right?"

Olivia nodded. "Yeah, something like

that. They help protect us and set our laws. No humans know about us, but with something Chayton is developing, there's a very good chance our laws will be changing soon."

"The serum, right?"

"Yes, exactly. If it does what he suspects, we'll be able to open our part of the world to others. We just have to figure out how without the world freaking out."

"Right, can you imagine the news? Tonight at ten, vampires come out of the closet and want to invite you for dinner!"

A laugh bubbled from Olivia's throat. "I don't imagine it going to be quite like that, but we'll see." She stood and checked her watch. "I'm not rushing you or anything like that, but Todd is downstairs waiting for you. You'll have my cell number if you need anything, or just want to talk."

Tawne reached for her friend and

pulled her close. She clung to her and closed her eyes. "I've never been so scared of anything in my entire life, and yet also liberated to experience this once in a lifetime encounter."

"Just be yourself," Olivia told her. "Now, as for Will, just give him time. I promise, he'll come around."

"I still can't believe I'm doing this."

Olivia lifted Sherlock into her arms and cradled her cat. "Think of this like winning the lottery. You will move into a mansion with four men who will do anything, be anything, for you. This would not be happening if they didn't want to do this with you."

"That includes Will?"

"Don't worry about Will. Now go, when you're ready, and have the time of your life!"

Tawne pulled her suitcase from the bed to the floor, then lifted the handle. "Walk me out?"

"Of course."

The two made their way toward the outer parking area and as Olivia had said, Todd was standing in wait by the passenger door. As soon as he saw them, he opened the door for her. When the dome light came on, her eyes widened. Inside sat Cristofano.

He lifted a glass toward her with a smile. A grin spread across her lips.

"Go get 'em," Olivia whispered.

One step in front of the other, Tawne made her way to the car. Todd took her bag and stood by the door.

"Are you ready?" Todd asked.

She nodded.

Cristofano leaned over on the seat and offered his hand. She slipped hers into his and slid into the car. The door closed behind her and she gasped. Evan sat next to Cristofano, Chayton next to him, and in a darkened corner of the limo, Will. Four men surrounded her and before she could speak or even think, the car sped off.

"We're glad you're coming to stay with us," Cristofano announced. He lifted a goblet filled with a bubbly substance and handed it over to her.

She brought it to her nose and sniffed. Champagne. Curious, she lifted her gaze to his. "Do you drink champagne?"

"I have, but prefer another source."

She lifted the glass to her lips and sipped. The bubbles tickled her tongue and the chill of the champagne slipped down her throat. She shifted her gaze over to Will. The vampire sat staring down at his hands, his brows furrowed.

"Is everyone happy with this arrangement?"

He looked up at her and frowned. She held his stare, not in a challenge, but in the hope he would at least say something. He seemed cold, distant, but the understanding wasn't there. She'd done nothing she was aware of for him to be ugly, or hateful.

They rode in an awkward silence for a few more seconds when Chayton spoke up.

"Well, I personally am happy you're coming with us. With everything that Olivia has spoken about you, I'm looking forward to getting to know you better. Everything you need will be provided, if we're not able to do it for you."

She smiled and folded her hands in her lap. Was this how Olivia felt in her car ride to her new home? She'd also been surrounded by strange men she had just met. Olivia has never looked happier.

This could be a future for her, if she allowed it to happen and accepted it. Four incredibly sexy-as-sin men were opening their lives for her. She wasn't a blood demon, but she was willing to give this a chance, just like they were with her.

"Thank you, Chayton. I'm looking forward to it as well. Call me excited, but I do have a few questions."

Cristofano leaned over and turned toward her, his arm coming to hover up next to her face. "We'll do our best to answer them." With a finger, he gently moved a few strands of hair from her face, then tucked them behind her ear. "You're a very beautiful woman, Tawne."

She smiled, and heat crept up her neck. She was thankful for the darkness of the car.

Can they see in the dark as if they were in the light? Probably. Just my luck.

"Do you feed on humans?"

"We have before," Cristofano answered.

She swallowed the lump in her throat. "Does it feed you like a blood demon would?"

"If it did, we wouldn't have the pairing ceremonies, now would we?" Will answered in a dry, sarcastic tone.

She lifted a brow and stared at him across the car. "Then why feed on humans?"

He met her gaze and like Cristofano, he leaned toward her. His lips pulled into a grin that was not welcoming, but frightening. Fear spiked in the back of her mind and a shiver rushed up her spine. She had not felt scared until this moment.

Danger Will Robinson! Danger!

"Because the hunt is fun and to feel the life force drain from their bodies is what we live for."

Her eyes widened, and she sat back in her seat. She was second guessing leaving the safety of Olivia's home for this new adventure.

Whack!

Will's head knocked forward and the man growled. It was worse than the grin. It was menacing and filled with rage.

"Don't talk to our guest like that," Evan snarled. "What the hell is wrong with you?"

"She's a fucking human and you want me to be okay with this?"

"Yes, we all do," Cristofano spouted back. "Apologize. Now."

"What for? She's a human and comes to us as a sort of pet!"

"I don't need this shit," she announced and wrapped her arms around her waist. "Bring me back to Olivia's house. Now. I'm not doing this."

Cristofano sighed and turned toward her once more. "Please, forgive my brother. He's an asshole. He has forgotten what it is like to be a human. Please, Tawne, don't leave us just yet. Give our arrangement a chance. Don't judge us based on the appearance of an asshole."

"Fuck you," Will growled and turned away from his audience. "I don't have to like this, and I choose not to participate."

"Fine by me," Tawne shot back at him.

He snapped a glare at her and snarled, showing his fangs, most likely for her benefit. "Just stay away from me."

"Fine. Stay away from me as well. I don't want asshole rubbing off on me. I sure as hell don't need an abusive prick putting me down. I've had plenty of those already." She turned away from him and shifted her attention to Cristofano. "I'm sorry, I'm normally not like this, but if we're going to do this, it needs to be you three. *Not* him."

Cristofano nodded and took her hand in his. He lifted it and pressed his lips to the back of her hand. "It was not our intention for any animosity or the like to happen."

"We wanted to try this with you, rather than spending time with a blood demon we have no connection with," Chayton added.

Evan leaned in and took her other hand. "There's something about you that we're all attracted to. Even if some of us have a hard time admitting it."

Tawne didn't want to look Will's way, but curiosity won out. She met his stare and he flashed his scrutiny in the other direction.

"I'm not able to put my finger on it just yet," Evan continued, "but with time, I hope to understand what it is."

The atmosphere in the car shifted from fury to contentment. She inhaled a deep breath and slowly, let it out. A subtle calm settled over her. She made a mental note to not venture toward Will's wing of the house, wherever that might be.

The limo took a turn and when the car slowed, she felt it maneuver over a bump. Her calmness faded in a rush when heightened nerves made her heartbeat quicken. They had arrived.

She fisted her hands by her side and

released them, over and over. She noticed Cristofano frown when he glimpsed her eyes. She had to assume he could not only sense her apprehension but also see it in the depths of her gaze despite how forcefully she attempted to hide it from him.

"As I promised, nothing will happen, take place, anything, without your consent," he reassured her.

She nodded and cleared her throat, forcing herself to calm. "I'm excited to begin this new adventure. I'm walking into a world I have only ever read about. I'm thrilled, no, elated, to be here with you. I only ask you to give me a minute to breathe."

Three of the four men nodded, almost in unison. She glanced over to Will and he reached for the handle when the car came to a stop. He made haste in scampering from the vehicle and she could hear his rapid footsteps fade in the distance.

She sighed and slid over to the open door. Glancing back at the vampires behind her, she met every set of eyes focused on her. She felt as if she were a baby deer in a darkened cave. Three sets of eyes were observing her, waiting to pounce when she turned her back.

I feel as if I'm learning how to swim at the deep end of the ocean, and I'm surrounded by sharks waiting to pounce on their next meal.

Tawne stepped out of the car and when she stood, she gasped. Before her was a mansion larger than she had ever seen on TV or the movies. Even the house Olivia was in was smaller than the one laid out before her.

A set of hands came to rest on her shoulders. "Welcome home," Cristofano whispered into her ear from behind her. "Let's go inside and we'll give you the tour, and show you to the room you'll be staying in."

Chapter Seven

IT WAS NOT everyday someone would hear the words, "Vampires are real."

Tawne stepped into the house through a set of double wooden doors. As she took her first few steps from the entrance, a grand foyer stretched before her. To the left appeared to be a library, or maybe a study. She could see the wall lined with books. She made a mental note to visit this area soon. To her right, a gathering room completely open with white walls, and against the wall, a baby grand piano. She smiled when she saw it. The black piano stood out in stark difference to the all white room.

"Do you play?" Evan asked her.

She shook her head. "No, I don't, but I've always wanted to learn."

"I'm sure we can arrange a lesson or two."

She turned to him and excitement raced through her. "You play?"

He shook his head. "I do not, but one of us has played for many years."

The house, like the gathering room, was white walled with art hung in a few places. She recalled the fountain in Olivia's home and wondered if they had one here as well.

"If you follow the hall, down on the right you'll find the kitchen," Cristofano told her. "We have someone on standby to cook as needed. We planned to have him here during your stay."

"That's great to hear. Thank you for

considering me."

"Of course," he told her. "Allow us to show you to where you'll sleep, then you're welcome to walk about the house and get yourself acclimated."

"Thank you. I'd like to do that."

Next to the gathering room stood a magnificent staircase. The arm rails gleamed golden. She wanted to touch them, but also didn't want to leave smudges.

"Is this real gold?"

A chuckle sounded behind her, and Tawne realized she asked this question out loud.

"I didn't mean, oh, I'm sorry. I didn't realize my thoughts were spoken. I kinda have a bad habit of doing that."

Chayton took a step toward her. "Even if it were gold, would it matter?"

She shook her head. "No, I suppose not."

He grinned. "Well, that's good. Because

it's not."

"Oh, okay. Good to know."

Chayton then added, "It's wood with a gold plating over it."

She lifted a brow. "Then that does make it gold."

"Not necessarily. If you took a piece of trash and dipped it in gold, would you have gold, or gold covered trash?"

She shrugged. "Honestly, it's still trash, but covered in gold. The value would go up, I would think."

Chayton took her hand and ascended the stairs. "If you say so, but to me, it's still trash. If something is carved from gold, it is gold throughout. However, if a monster is covered in gold, it is still a monster, just wearing gold to cover the rough outer exterior and hardness of the original design. Now, let's go find your room."

She thought about what he said, and a few past relationships came to mind.

Brian who thought what he wanted and demanded from her was far more important than what she could ever hope for. Nothing she ever said or did mattered. That relationship was over before it started.

Then there was David. He came in suave and seductive, then turned out to be an abusive asshole; even more so when he drank.

If you dipped a monster in gold, it is still a monster.

She grinned and gave a side-glance to Chayton. "Thank you."

He smiled. "For what?"

She squeezed his hand and stood at the top of the stairs to the second floor. "For being honest. And for calling something shit when it's still shit, even if it's covered in gold."

He raised his brows. "Because it's still shit?"

She laughed with a nod. "Exactly."

Chayton smiled. "There is also an elevator in our home. If you'd rather take it, consider it yours."

"Really? Wow. I'll definitely think about it." Tawne turned her attention to the room in front of her. She thought taking the stairs up would have led her to a hallway of bedrooms, or something with doors. She didn't expect to walk into a split room.

One side held a few crimson couches with matching curtains. A chandelier of crystal hung in the middle of the room. In the far corner sat a cello by wing chairs, a wooden coffee, and a few end tables.

Someone here plays cello? A piano and a cello. What's next? Violin or drums? I will have my own orchestra!

The other room had a large red carpet in the middle with two white couches on either end of it. Against the far wall a bar with all types of liquors lined up for consumption. She imagined a Christmas tree in the middle of the room on the red carpet with many presents tucked underneath it.

"These rooms are beautiful." Tawne turned around to face the men.

Chayton leaned against the wall. "Thank you."

Evan and Cristofano took a few steps closer to her. The three of them surrounded her where she stood, but not in a menacing way. More of a protective stance. If she were to fall, they would catch her. Well, all except for Will. He'd probably let her fall on her ass.

I have to get to know him better, find out what makes him tick. And why he's such an asshole.

She pointed across the room to the cello. "Do any of you play?"

"Yes, same one who plays the piano," Cristofano answered.

She turned to him with a raised brow.

"May I ask who it is?"

"That would be Will," Evan answered.

Her mouth opened in shock. She didn't know him, but he didn't seem the type to play music. He was so cold. "He plays the cello?"

Cristofano nodded. "And the piano and many other musical instruments."

"I find that surprising."

"There are many things about all of us that may surprise you." Chayton motioned toward the stairs. "Shall we continue?"

"Yes." The coldest one in the house played music. She found this surprising, and intriguing. Did Will have this hard exterior that took a chisel to get through? Was he the soft teddy bear on the inside? A smile tugged the corner of her mouth. She wasn't sure, but it was something to find out. The one who pushed those away usually had the thickest of walls to climb over and get through. However, once the walls were conquered, there was a whole other person on the inside, waiting to be discovered.

Challenge accepted.

Continuing up the stairs to the third level, the hall she'd expected to see on the second floor extended before her. To her right, a few doors and even other hallways. Who stayed down there and where did the other hallways lead to?

To her left, more doors and at the end, a sitting room with four tan wing chairs surrounding a round coffee table.

Along each hall hung portraits, either depicting people or wildlife. It reminded her of her time spent at the museum in downtown New Orleans. There was a nudge of excitement in wanting to know more about all the art; the portraits and other photographs, the vases, and the sculptures downstairs.

She stepped into the cavernous sitting room, glanced up to the ceiling and smiled at the openness of it. Skylights were installed into the roofing and she made a mental note to come out here during the night to behold the stars, or even the rain and storms.

"Down here is your room," Cristofano announced in the silence.

She turned and followed Cristofano down the right side of the corridor. He stopped in front of the first door on the left, turned the knob, and pushed the door open.

Tawne stepped inside and the light instantly turned on.

"Motion sensors," he told her. "They don't work if you turn off the power to the room."

She barely heard what he said due to the beauty of the room captivating her.

The walls were a champagne color with curtains and valance in the windows of similar but darker hue. The windows were huge, floor to ceiling in height. The ceiling held another chandelier. Across the room sat a fireplace underneath a bone white mantle. Crystal candleholders stood on either side, and a gold framed mirror above it.

A chaise lounge was in the corner by the windows with a few other matching sitting chairs. Then there was the bed. King size, dark mahogany, with window valance and curtains behind it, framing the bed, and what looked like at least twenty pillows strewn across the headboard. A smoky-gray, tempered glass table with two sitting chairs graced the area at the end of the bed.

She felt like a princess waking up from a long sleep to a world she had no memory of living in.

"There's a closet with some of your clothes. We took the liberty of ordering a few pieces for your stay here. You're welcome to utilize anything in this room or throughout the house. Please, consider it yours."

She turned to Cristofano and fingers covered her mouth with her fingers, hoping to keep in a squeal. She lowered them quickly. "All of this is mine?" she whispered.

He chuckled. "So long you wish to stay, yes, it's all yours."

She shook her head and slowly spun in a circle. "I don't even know where to begin with all of this. You're asking me to stay here with you, knowing I could never give you what you need. Why?" She turned to face the three men in the room.

Cristofano and Evan turned to Chayton.

"What happened?" Tawne asked. "I feel like there's a big elephant in the room here and I'm the only one not seeing it."

"There's no elephant," Cristofano offered. "There is something Chayton is working on, though."

"Yes," Chayton said and took a step

forward. "I am working on something I think will be life changing for not only vampires, but for humans as well." He pressed the tips of his fingers together. "Recall the conversation about the serum I said I was working on?" She nodded and Chayton continued. "Well, if I'm successful in what I'm wanting to achieve with it, there's a potential it will give you the same blood type as a Blood Demon, without becoming said demon. This would be along the lines of a miracle cure-all for all vampires today, and our future lines. During the trial phase of it, I want to test it on you and see how your blood reacts."

The excitement of staying in this amazing room inside this remarkable home began to fade. She felt like a prize that had been trapped in a pretty box. She was an experiment? Was this the only reason they wanted her to be here?

Tawne took a step forward and placed

her hands on her hips. "All right. I thought I knew why I was here, but now, I'm not sure. Please, do tell. Am I here as an experiment? Am I some type of test subject? Because I will tell you right here and now, that is not what I signed up for. If you think for a second you can inject me with some sort of crazy fuck-all and think I'll be okay with it, you can think again!"

Chayton held his hands up in surrender. "Tawne, I promise you, you are not here as a test subject. When Olivia told us about you, we were all intrigued and wanted to meet you."

"That's correct," Cristofano added. "She showed us pictures of you two together, the life you shared as friends."

"And when Olivia told us she let you in on our part of the world," Evan offered and took a few steps toward her. "You didn't flinch, not once. It takes a strong individual to accept a new world like ours, but an even braver one to take it head on with no fear."

"I appreciate all of this, and what you're saying, but what is in this for me? I don't mean to sound ungrateful. It's not that at all. You need a blood demon to survive. I'm not a blood demon. I'm a human. I'm not sure what the catch is."

"There is no catch," Cristofano said.

"Oh no, there is. Tell her what it is," came a new voice.

Tawne turned and watched as Will stepped into the room. He wore a dark gray t-shirt with a popular brand name on the front, and had his hands shoved into his denim pockets. He met Tawne's alarmed gaze and smirked.

"Tell her what you plan to do with her and how you want to change the face of all things vampires. Tell her how you want to be the person who makes it possible for vampires to be out in the open. Better yet, tell her she'll be nothing more than a pet to be shared between you all for a few good fucks."

Her eyes widened at his words and she took a few steps toward him. "How dare you! I am no one's pet and certainly no fuck toy. Now, you can just turn around and leave this room, and never speak to me again! Who do you think you are, coming in here, talking to me like I'm a piece of trash? You know nothing about me!"

Will met her halfway and his chest almost bumped into her body. She fumed and was ready to fight. She didn't care he was much taller, stronger, more deadly, sinfully-sexy-as-hell, but, dammit, she hated him right now.

"You are a human. I am a vampire. In a pyramid of dominance, you, my pet, are on the bottom." Will traced a finger across her cheek, down her neck. He slipped his hand around her throat and leaned in.

Fear clamped down on her and she took a step back. Will grabbed her by the back of her hair and yanked her head back, exposing her neck.

"Will, dammit, leave her be. She did nothing to deserve this," Cristofano yelled out.

Tawne's breath came in spurts and her heart beat hard in her chest. She pressed her hands against his chest, but he wasn't moving. "Let me the fuck go!"

"No," he growled. "Do you fantasize about being bitten? Being fucked by four cocks at once? Is that what you want? You want us to ravage your body?"

"No!" She struggled against his grip and felt like a rag doll in his grasp. "Let me go!"

"Let her go," Chayton said in a low, commanding tone. "Now, or you'll fight me."

Will shifted his glare to the man next to him and snarled. He let Tawne go and she fell on her backside. "Fine, have it your way, but I'm not taking part in your little experiment of human blood tasting." He peered down at Tawne once more, and for a single moment, she thought she saw sadness in his eyes.

A tear slipped down her cheek and Will closed his eyes. "Why do you hate me? You don't even know me," she whispered.

Will's body slumped when he sighed and opened his eyes. He stared down at Tawne and furrowed his brows. "I don't hate you. I just don't like you." He turned to leave the room when Tawne spoke up.

"But, why? What did I ever do to you? You don't know me."

He paused in the doorway and turned to regard her over his shoulder. The other three vampires helped her to her feet. Chayton swiped the tear from her cheek.

Tawne waited for an answer and when one didn't come, she pulled loose from the men. She inhaled a deep breath, then released it as she crossed the room. She stood next to Will and raised a hand to touch his arm, then stopped and lowered it back to her side. "I don't know what happened to you, but I'm sorry. I wish I could take away your pain but taking it out on me is not fair. I didn't do anything to you and don't deserve the backlash I just received. But, Will?" She looked up and stared into his hard, cold eyes. "I forgive you."

Tawne lowered her head and looked at the floor. She'd turned to leave him when Will grabbed her by the arm. She stopped and looked over her shoulder at him.

Will opened his mouth to say something, then closed it once more. He shook his head and let her go. He left the room, his footsteps fading as he trekked down the hall. In the distance, she heard a door slam.

She turned to the others in the room

and met their stares, one by one. "If we're going to do this, we all need to be honest with each other. Chayton, what is it you're developing? How will it affect me and your community? I want to help, but I need to know everything."

Cristofano nodded and took a step forward. "You're right, and we'll give all of what you need to know once you've spent time with us. We know only what Olivia has told us. I can speak for my brothers here, that we are intrigued and want to know more, and need you, Tawne. We are looking for someone to handle all four of us, and if it's any indicator with how you just handled yourself with Will, I believe you are the one for us."

His words, as sincere as they were, did not completely convince her this was where she needed to be. Tawne wanted someone to call her own, someone to look at her like she was the last breath they would need to survive. She wanted someone to captivate her in a way that would forever rock her to her core. Three of four men were offering this world to her, if she was brave enough to accept it.

She wanted this, and even if that meant getting close to Will, she would do it. She wanted in on this secret world. She longed for a new adventure. The universe had spoken, loud and clear. Now it was up to her on what her next step would be.

Tawne crossed her arms over her chest and held her head high. "All right. I'm in."

Chapter Eight

ALL RIGHT, I'M in.

Tawne kept replaying the conversation between her, Will, and the others in her mind, over and over again.

What did I just agree to?

The men had left her alone in her room to unpack, change clothes, relax, bathe, sleep, whatever she felt like doing. Right now, she wanted to scout the house for exits, entrances, where everyone's rooms were, and if there was a pool. A house this size had to have some sort of pool or hot tub, or both.

She crossed her new bedroom to the windows. Each were trimmed with champagne valances that had to cost as much as a month's salary at the museum. Probably more. Pulling one to the side, she found a handle on what appeared to be a window type door. She turned it, opened the glass pane, and stepped outside.

Warmth welcomed her as the sun began to set for the day. She closed her eyes and lifted her face to the fading light. She planned on taking in all she could until she was met with the rising moon. Since vampires did not venture out into the sun, she didn't expect to be out here much; however, she would have to be sure to get out here occasionally to soak up the rays.

A breeze blew, and it shifted her hair across her back, tickling her exposed arms. She sighed and opened her eyes once more, then smiled at the landscape surrounding her view.

A pond in the distance had a fountain sprinkling water into the pool below, and a few ducks and a swan were swimming through the rippling water with ease. Trees surrounded the outer edges of the property en mass. If there was a fence around the property line, she wasn't aware, but couldn't imagine a place like this not having some type of security.

The thought of security brought another thought to mind. What if she wanted to leave for an outing? Could she? Would they let her, or would she be escorted? Hopefully the former, but most likely the latter. Close to her balcony, She spied a swing big enough to hold three people. It was wooden and reminded her of the park downtown.

She walked back inside and closed the door behind her. She wanted to tour the home on her own and decided right now would be the best time to start. Making her way to her door, she grabbed the doorknob and paused for a moment.

When Will left earlier, I heard a door slam in the distance. Is his room up here as well? If so, which one would belong to him?

Touring the house didn't include stumbling into someone's room. She could imagine that conversation.

Oh, hi, Will. No, I wasn't snooping. I was just checking what was behind door number three.

She opened her door and stepped out, this time with her eyes open. She didn't want a repeat of Will walking up on her blind. She pulled the door closed and went back the way they came in toward the staircase. She glanced down over the railing at the steps and could see the gathering rooms on the second floor, and the main entry on the first floor. Was there a basement? A courtyard?

I need to find out if there's a pool. They also said something about an elevator.

She looked to her right and found an elegant, dark oak desk pushed against the window with paper and a quill sitting on a corner of it. Walking over to it, she touched the writing pen and smiled. It wasn't often ink wells and writing quills were out for use. The sound of gears moving broke the silence. She glanced over her shoulder and found the elevator door and a backlit panel with buttons. Giving herself a nod for finding it, she turned back toward the stairs and paused. Her room was to the left, somewhere down on the right was Will's.

The line from the children's movie, *don't go near the west wing,* rang through her mind. She suddenly felt like the carpenter's daughter held captive by a beast who wanted to torment her, but there was another side to the man, a side she wanted to find.

She took the stairs down to the second floor. The familiar rooms were in view, but there had to be more. Walking through the room where the Cello was placed, she noticed it extended to another room with a pool table, foosball, and a two lane bowling alley.

She raised her brows at this extravagance and stepped inside the room. She'd played pool before, some foosball, but bowling wasn't something she excelled at. She grinned at the thought of the four vampires in this house all bowling.

Turning around to walk back, she observed a bar behind her. With its shiny mirrored backing flashing her reflection as she made her way closer to the wooden slab top, she discovered the bar was filled with liquor and flavors. How much alcohol was needed in one home was uncertain, but who was she to judge? She felt thirsty, so why not make a drink? Stepping behind the bar, she picked up a glass and pushed the sliding lid for the ice.

No ice.

"What kind of bar has no ice?"

"The kind that isn't used often," Cristofano answered.

She gasped and jumped back. "Shit, you scared me. I thought I was alone."

"Oh, you were, but I felt your presence. I hope you don't mind?"

"My presence?" She shook her head. "No, I don't mind. How did you feel my presence?"

"It's a vampire thing we do. We pick up on emotions. I can feel you on another floor."

She raised her brows. "Everyone can pick up on me?"

He nodded. "Or they can choose to ignore it. I asked the lot to leave you be for a while."

She smiled and picked up her glass.

"So why did you come then?"

He shrugged. "I was hoping to help settle any doubts, fears, or maybe get you a drink?"

She tilted the glass and tapped the side of it with her finger. "No ice."

"What are you wanting to make?"

"Hmm, vodka tonic."

He nodded. "There's vodka in the freezer and tonic in the fridge. You shouldn't need ice for that."

"Oh." She turned and opened the freezer and sure enough, a bottle of Vodka sat in the door. She grabbed it then found the tonic. She poured the drink, half and half. If today was any indication of how things would progress, she needed a strong drink.

"Do you like your room?"

She met his gaze while drinking. Setting the glass down, she licked her upper lip, then nodded. "Yes, very much so. It's beautiful." When Cristofano didn't say anything or move, she raised a brow. "Are you all right?" He was staring at her mouth, unmoving.

"What?" He met her gaze, then smiled and shifted the weight on his feet. "Yes, I'm fine. I was mesmerized by the flick of your tongue over your lips."

A heat rushed through her and her face burned. She grinned and lowered her gaze to the ground. "No one has ever said anything like that to me before."

"No one has seen you the way we do, Tawne."

She wasn't sure how it happened, but Cristofano stood directly in front of her. She looked up at the man staring into her eyes. He lifted his hand and with a gentle touch, slipped his finger across her cheek and down to trace over her neck where her pulse point throbbed. "You are most exquisite."

Her breath hitched, her knees felt weak, and a warmth kindled between her legs. The glass in her hand suddenly felt heavy.

"You missed a spot," he whispered. "May I?"

Her body ignited in a full flame of desire. Would he lick her mouth? Kiss her? Both? She wanted to throw herself on him and do naughty, awful things to him. No one had ever brought her to orgasm, and the only ones she'd experienced previously were given by her own doings. However, with Cristofano and his brothers, she imagined losing count of the times she would come for them.

"Tawne?"

"Hmm?"

"May I?"

She realized she hadn't said anything or moved. She parted her lips and whispered, "Yes."

Cristofano took the drink from her hand and set it down on the bar. He brought up his hands and held both sides of her face. He tilted her head up just slightly, then leaned in. She closed her eyes and a whisper of a kiss brushed just next to her mouth, then another slightly above her lips.

Tawne fisted her hands and could feel the self-control slipping. She reached up for Cristofano and gripped his arms at the bend of his elbow. His muscles flexed and contracted against her fingers. "You taste of the sun, vodka, and magic."

"Will you let me taste you as well?" The words were out before she realized what she asked.

A chuckle bubbled from Cristofano. "Yes, I would love that."

Without hesitation, Tawne lifted up on her toes and tilted her head up. She slanted her mouth over his and a groan passed between them. Cristofano tilted her head back and slipped his tongue over her lips, pushing them apart. His tongue darted inside, grazing over her teeth and tangling with her tongue.

She wasn't sure what to expect when kissing a vampire, but by all accounts, this was the best kiss she had ever experienced. He took his time seducing her mouth with his. He slipped his tongue out and teased her lips before dipping back in. He pulled her closer against his body with one hand around her waist and the other buried into her hair.

Then, he broke away from her. Resting his forehead against her, he panted. "Tawne, forgive me. I have been wanting to do that since we met."

"No apologies are needed. I wanted you to kiss me as well."

"I'm afraid I've taken you from your tour of our home, though."

She opened her eyes and pulled back to look into his. "Not at all, but, let's take a moment." She reluctantly pulled herself free from his grasp and took a step back. She wiped at her lower lip, then picked up her drink. She took a long sip, then cleared her throat. "Tell me about you. What did you do in your human life that brought you to where you are now?"

He motioned to the bar stools. The two took a seat. Cristofano fiddled with a few napkins on the bar as he spoke. "I was born and raised in Venice. I lived near the Bridge of Sighs, or *Ponte Dei Sospiri.* Occasionally, at night, in the wind I could hear the whispers of those long ago captured and sent to *Prigioni Nuove,* or The New Prison. The whispers were always greater near the Doge's palace.

"I fought in the wars between Venice and Italy. After the third Independence War in 1866, Venice finally joined in with Italy. Most did not want to do it, but what could you do? It was not like here in the states. You lived, or you died trying to leave.

"When I turned twenty-nine, I left and joined the military. It was there that I picked up on investments. I served my time in our army, then left. I ventured out to work with money and understand how to invest it. It was at that point that I met the man who changed my life."

Cristofano paused for a moment, as if reflecting. Tawne sipped on her vodka tonic and waited patiently for him to continue.

"I met a man who had a lot of money he'd inherited and wanted to invest. So, we talked for a while, we shared a few drinks, and when it was time to seal the deal, he turned on me. He attacked me in an alley. It was dark and no one else was around. The last thing I remember, he stabbed me in the gut and then my chest. He threatened something about taking all of my money and investments. Just as I dropped to the ground to die, a sound erupted in the alley that would have frightened me if I were not already dying.

"A second later, the man who attacked me was thrown from where he stood. I heard him scream, then everything was silent. A shadow fell over me as I blacked out. I thought I had died, until I woke with an intense thirst the likes of which I had never felt before."

Cristofano toyed with the fangs in his mouth as she watched him relive the moment he woke as a vampire.

"Did it hurt?"

He met her stare, then shook his head. "Not in the least. My maker stayed with me for a while, and when I was ready he released me. I decided to stay with investments; it's what I knew. I started up my own firm and needed someone to run the place with me. That's where I met Evan and Will."

She could not move from her seat. "I love history and my dream is to become a museum curator. Your story of Venice, the war, the Doge's palace..." she trailed off and smiled like a kid on a sugar high. "I would love to hear more when you're up to sharing."

"Sure, anytime. I enjoy your company."

She reached for his hand and squeezed it. "And I yours."

"Did I hear my name?"

Another voice joined their conversation and Tawne smiled as Evan stepped into the game room.

"Ahh, I see my time alone with you has come to an end. However, I'm happy to hand you over to Evan." Cristofano lifted her hand to his mouth and pressed his lips firmly on the back of her hand. He kept his gaze fixed on hers as he reluctantly lowered her hand to rest on the edge of the bar. "I look forward to our time together again." Cristofano leaned in and a kiss as soft as a rose petal breathed across her cheek. *Addio per ora, bella signora.*"

"What does that mean?" she whispered.

"I'll tell you later," he winked and moved away. "Evan, my brother, enjoy your time with our beautiful guest."

Evan grinned and stepped further into the room, around the departing Cristofano. "It would be my pleasure."

Tawne followed Cristofano with her gaze as he left the room. As soon as he was out of sight, she turned her attention to Evan. "Well, hello there," she said with a grin.

Chapter Nine

IN NORMAL SITUATIONS, dating took place between one man and one woman. Ending her time with Cristofano, at least for the moment, she almost felt as if she were cheating on him with Evan. However, in this instance, the cheating was non-existent, and the men encouraged her to get to know each of them. She made a mental note that time with Will would happen. If this arrangement was meant to be, the two of them would need to meet somewhere on level playing ground.

The men were brothers at arms and she was a woman between all four of them. She still as not quite sure how to handle this knowledge, but in time, it would come to her.

Evan crossed the room toward her in a dark gray, pinstriped suit, white shirt, and black tie. His hair was on the longer side, styled in the current style men wore: thick wave on top and set back. His olive skin tone and light blue eyes were striking, alluring, and sinful.

His sculpted chin with the coarse beard growth cut close to his face, made her think of the abrasions he would leave on her thighs and she felt a heat rise up her throat and into her cheeks even as her core set to a consistent throbbing.

He smiled, flashing those perfect white teeth with a set of razor sharp vampire fangs. He was the epitome of a sex god. Hell, all four of them were sex gods who walked this earth.

Evan pushed his hands into his pockets and stopped just in front of her. "I hope the visit with Cris went well?"

She nodded and took note of the nickname he used for Cristofano. She still wasn't used to hearing it, nor felt familiar enough with him to use it yet. Soon, though. "Yes, very well." Tawne linked her hands together and brought them to rest in her lap. "You seem to know more about me, than I do about you. Please, I'd love to hear your story if you're willing to share it?"

"Of course." Evan motioned to the barstools in the room. She felt his hand as he brushed it over the lower part of her back.

"May I have another vodka tonic?"

He took her glass. "Of course." He walked around the bar and made the drink for her, then sat it down. "How far back would you like me to go?"

She lifted the drink to her lips and sipped on the contents, the vodka burning slightly down her throat. "As far as you're willing to go."

He lowered his eyes for a moment and fiddled with the glasses.

Tawne rested her elbows on the bar.

He sighed and met her gaze. "During the twenties, I spent much of my time in a speakeasy. Times were hard, but liquor sales were harder. I smuggled much of what came in and out of New York City. I smoked, drank, and fucked my way through the city until I found myself out of options. I burned most, if not all of my bridges. I wasn't a good person back then." His brows rose as he talked. "If I wasn't smuggling, I was drinking. If I wasn't drinking, I was fucking. If I wasn't with a whore, I was looking for my next hit."

Tawne leaned forward and rested her head on her hand and listened to his story. She hoped he would share some of his past but having only spent a day or so with Evan, she didn't expect this.

He lowered his gaze back to the bar. "Eventually, it all caught up with me. One of the right hands of the mafia caught wind of my whereabouts. He brought me in and I had my ass handed to me. I was left for dead in my hotel room with several stab wounds, my legs both broken in several places, a severe concussion along with broken ribs."

"Holy shit," she whispered.

He looked at her again. "I was close to death when room service found me. I woke in the morgue. Apparently they thought I was dead. The man who worked that night in the morgue changed my life entirely. He was not a vampire, but a blood demon. When the authorities brought me in, throwing me on a cold metal table in for an autopsy, he realized I still had a faint pulse. He waited until everyone else had left and then called upon his vampire lady friend. The rest, we will say, is history."

"Oh my god." Tawne leaned against the bar and shook her head. "I'm not even sure what to ask at this point. The story of your transition sounds...tragic."

He nodded. "It was. I didn't want this life. Hell, I didn't want my human life, either. But when Malik found me, he changed everything."

She furrowed her brows, curious, she asked, "Who is Malik?"

He smiled. "You'll meet him soon enough. Think of him as our governor."

"Okay, so what happened when Malik found you?"

"He introduced me to Cris. He took me in and we became something like brothers. Malik helped me understand what my new life meant, but it was Cris who saved me."

"That's wonderful to hear."

"From that point, I no longer struggled with my identity. As a smuggler of booze, I was great with numbers. So, rather than importing illegal goods, I became an accountant. I work for the coven, our group here, and a few outside I've met along the way."

"And here I am, interested in history, and learning about a different era I've never been involved in. I'm completely fascinated. I hope you'll share more of your life with me?"

He nodded. "Absolutely. In time, we'll know everything there is about one another." He winked and Tawne grinned.

"May I ask a question?"

"You may ask anything."

"Why would the four of you want to share one woman?"

He smirked. "It is something we've wanted for as far back as I can remember. The coven brought the idea to the table, and many opted in for it. Not everyone agrees, but not everyone matters."

She grinned. "I agree with that. When Olivia told me about her arrangement with her men, I had a hard time believing it."

"Why? If I may ask?"

"Sure. I suppose because it's hard for me to believe five men can love one woman, while she loves all of them in return. No jealousy, no fighting, nothing."

"I won't lie to you, Tawne. This arrangement can be hard. Each of us have our own personality, traits, and flaws. Each of us will want one on one time with you. We will also want to be with you all at once."

She felt the heat race up her body once more. "I can't imagine being with more than one person a time," she whispered.

"You would be surprised what the body wants. No one will push you into that situation; no one will make you do anything you're not comfortable with. However, to be in this relationship, it comes with all of us."

"You four and me, no one else?"

He nodded. "No one else."

"Why do I feel like I'm the selfish one and getting all the candy in the store?"

He chuckled. "Because our candy is specially made just for you."

She bit her bottom lip and smirked. "Aren't I the lucky girl?"

Evan walked around the bar and unbuttoned his dress jacket. Tawne followed him with her gaze and smiled at the jukebox he stopped in front of. She had completely missed this when she first stepped inside the game room. Then again, she had been preoccupied with Cristofano.

He pressed a few buttons and a familiar song began to play. The instrumental intro brought a giggle from Tawne. Evan began to move to the beat of the song. When the singer started in, the song name and band finally clicked. It was *Gimme Some Lovin'* by *The Spencer Davis Group.*

Tawne turned her stool toward Evan and wondered if he would have her dance. What happened next caught her completely by surprise.

Evan took a step back, then spun around twice, feet wide, then snapped them together. He sang out loud with the song and cross the room to her, dancing the entire way.

She laughed and slid off her stool. Evan took her by the hands and twirled her under his arm, then back into his body. He took her hand and led her through the open space of the game.

"When did you learn to dance?"

"During the twenties, baby. It wasn't called roaring twenties for nothing, you know?"

She laughed, and he twirled her

around again. "I wasn't sure what to expect, but this was definitely not it. You've completely surprised me, Evan, in the most amazing way!"

He chuckled and pulled her closer to his frame. "There are many things I'm positive I could surprise you with."

She raised her brows. "Oh, do tell. I am but a humble servant."

He chuckled, then as the song began to fade, another began in its place. The telltale rhythm of the introduction did not go past her. *Percy Sledge* yelled out, *When a Man Loves a Woman*, and Tawne relaxed into Evan's arms. His cheek rested atop her head and the two slow danced in small, silken movements.

"Do you know how long it has been since I've dance like this with a man?"

"If you need to ask me, then it's been too long. I'm happy to have made you happy tonight."

She looked up at him and their gazes

met. Often when couples stare at one another, it tends to become a power play—who will yield first? In this moment though, it was different. She didn't want to look away, and neither did Evan. Well, if the seductive stare of his was any indication.

Evan brought her hand close and placed a soft kiss on the backside. He closed his eyes and held it there for a moment. "You are an exquisite woman, Tawne O'Brien." He met her gaze once more. "I look forward to getting to know you more intimately."

Her knees weakened and at the same time, Evan's arm around her waist tightened. If she were to fall, he would no doubt catch her. This brought her a feeling of safety, something she had not felt in a long time.

"Kiss me," she whispered.

He released her hand and slid his finger across the line of her jaw. Slipping his hand behind her head, he cradled her neck and leaned in. His lips slanted over hers in a soft, delicate kiss.

Tawne fisted her hand in his dress jacket and pulled him closer, hoping he would take her hint of needing more.

And he did. Evan slid his tongue across her lips. She opened for him and his mouth seduced hers in a dance of an erotic tease. Her panties were wet with need and soon, she would need a release of her own will.

She slipped her tongue into his mouth and it slid over the sharp edge of his fangs. The fact that he was a vampire had been long forgotten until the slight ting of pain reminded her. It did not stop her, though. She still needed more.

A groan erupted between them and she melted in his embrace.

"That was the most erotic thing I've ever heard," he mumbled against her lips.

"What?" she whispered.

"You groaned and it's taking everything I have to not lay you across the pool table right now."

"Holy shit," she giggled. "That was me?"

He grinned against her lips with a nod. "Yes, ma'am."

Tawne pulled back just slightly. "Well, thank you for not getting scared when that happened. I didn't even realize that was me."

He chuckled. "It turned me on even more." He leaned in and whispered. "Do it again."

The heat between her legs lit aflame with need. She bit her lower lip and grinned. "I can't do it on command, but I promise, it will definitely happen again."

He groaned and lolled his head back, feigning pain from her denial. "You scar me woman, you hurt me with your words." She giggled, and Evan brought his head back up with a smirk. "Oh look, all better." He twirled her once more and Tawne's laugh echoed throughout the game room.

She'd loved this time with Evan and enjoyed his personality. He was serious, yet, a complete goofball. He had been through so much in his life, yet never let it affect him. Many people in the world could take note from this man, including herself.

"I could do this every day and never tire of it," she announced.

"Then I shall make note to bring you here, every single day, for a dance, my love."

The words 'my love' did not go unnoticed. She slipped her hands up his chest, his pectorals flexing underneath her touch. She pushed her fingers into the back of his hair, playing with his tendrils. "I would love that."

The song had long since ended, and

another began to play, but she paid it no mind. All she wanted in this world were the men in this house, Evan's arms around her, and Cristofano's lips on hers.

Soon, she would spend time with Chayton and she would add another name to her list of desires. She wondered if that list would also include Will? Only time would tell at this point. Right now, this man captivated her attention.

"May I cut in?"

She turned to the familiar voice of Chayton and grinned.

"You may absolutely cut in, my brother," Evan answered. He turned Tawne to face him once more. "Until later, my love." He touched her chin with a single finger and lifted her face up. Leaning in, he slipped one more kiss across her lips, and teased the crease of her mouth with his tongue.

Evan let her go and Tawne took a step

back. She let out a long breath and shook her head. "You're evil," she whispered.

"You love it," he told her.

She shrugged with a smirk, then turned to face Chayton. "Hello there."

He lifted a brow and a smile stretched across his sexy-as-sin face. "Come on. I'd like to show you want I'm working on."

She looked back at Evan once more. "Thank you for a wonderful time."

"You're welcome. Until next time." Evan buttoned his dress jacket and turned to leave the room.

She turned back to Chayton and smiled. "Are we going to your evil laboratory?"

He chuckled and held a hand out for her. "Only if you agree to wear the goggles that come with it being evil."

Tawne laughed and slipped her hand into his. "Lead the way, evil overlord."

She wasn't sure how much time had

passed, between getting to know Cristofano, dancing with Evan, and now playing evil scientist with Chayton, but she would need to rest soon, and reflect over everything she'd learned.

She also wondered if today's tour of the lab would come with being seduced by a beaker or kissed by a burning flame. She didn't care, so long as she felt comfortable in her settings. The only concern she had with that was Will.

Chapter Ten

CHAYTON HELD ONTO Tawne's hand and they made their way toward the elevator. He wanted to show her what he had been working on, and she found herself curious. What made someone become a research doctor rather than working with patients? Being a vampire probably had a lot to do with that.

The end of the hall held the frame for the elevator. He pressed the down button and turned to face her. "We could take the stairs, but it's four flights. This might be faster. And gives you an idea where the elevator is on each floor."

She nodded. "I appreciate that."

The familiar ding announced the lift's arrival and the doors slid open. He held his hand out for her and she stepped inside. The interior was cream colored with mirrored handrails and a mirrored ceiling. Chayton pressed the B button and the doors closed.

"Do you spend a lot of time in your lab?"

He shook his head. "No, not all of my time. Well, most often as of late only because of what I'm working on. I'm excited to show it to you."

She smiled. "What is it?"

"It may be easier to show you than to explain, but once we're down there, you'll understand. Well, at least I hope you will."

She tilted her head, curious. "What about it would I not understand?" She didn't sound rude or condescending, the opposite actually. What was he working on that would be easier to see than to hear about?

The elevator arrived at the basement level and the doors opened.

Tawne had the thought of something like a mad scientist's laboratory in her mind, however, when the doors opened, it was a different sight completely. It was as if she'd walked into a white- walled department store of glass beakers filled with colorful perfumes. Different shapes and sizes, each contained a different color liquid. From blue to pink, to yellow and red, the kaleidoscope of colors was beautiful.

The lab had the distinctive scent of alcohol and cleaning products, similar to a hospital. It was cooler than the rest of the house she had visited. She shivered and wrapped her arms around herself.

"Here," Chayton offered and grabbed a

floor length, white lab jacket. He held it open. She turned around and he slipped it up her arms.

"Thank you." She pulled it tight around her body, reveling in the immediate small relief it offered, and turned back to face him. "Why is it so cold in here?"

"It keeps the germs and bacteria from growing. They can contaminate and we can't have that."

"Right, well makes sense. So, where is this thing you're working on?"

Chayton grinned and his eyes lit with excitement. "It is something that we all feel will completely change the face of our world. I'm working on perfecting a serum, well, more like a bonding agent."

The only serum's Tawne was familiar with were sold by makeup companies or for hair damage. "That sounds pretty important, considering it could change things. Can you give me for specifics?"

"Sure." He pulled out a stool for her by one of the tables.

She took a seat and placed her hands in her lap. In front of her were a few of the colorful vials. "These are beautiful colors."

He smiled and picked up a vial, then took a seat next to her. "Before I go into details about this serum, would you like to know more about me?"

She nodded with a smile. "Yes, absolutely. I was hoping you would share, either now or later."

"Good." He placed the vial into a metal holder. "Originally, I'm from Minnesota. My family is Sioux and, unfortunately, there are not many of us, my tribe, left. There was a war in the 1800's I fought in. My tribe fought to keep our land, but it was a losing battle. One night, one of the soldiers snuck into our camp and into my home." Chayton looked at his hands. "It was that night my maker attacked me.

I fought back, though. I won the fight, but it was also my undoing.

"The man bit me during our fight. At one point, he had me pinned to the ground and forced his blood into my mouth. I grabbed my hatchet and killed him, but it was already too late. The blood was in my system. My human body died that night and I was reborn as a vampire."

"Oh my god," she whispered. "I can't even imagine what that must have been like for you."

"It still haunts me from time to time, but I've learned to deal with it and forgive my past. If I didn't, I wouldn't have the life I do now with my brothers."

She reached for his hand and squeezed it. "Thank you for sharing your story."

"You're welcome." He picked up the vial and held it out to her.

She accepted the small glass tube and

examined the crimson contents. It was thick, like blood. "What is this?"

"It's the serum."

She smirked and lifted a brow. "Well, I figured that. What is it exactly?"

He winked then chuckled. "The serum I've been working on, think of it like a bonding agent, like I said before."

She nodded. "Okay, what does it do?"

Chayton grinned and his eyes gleamed with triumph. "This serum will bond to the blood of a human and transform their genetic makeup into synthetic blood."

She blinked. "Wait, what? Are you saying that this substance in this tube will make me a blood demon?"

"Yes and no."

She handed the vial back. "I'm... I don't know, Chayton. I'm not ready to be a test subject to see if this will work."

He chuckled. "I would never put you through any kind of testing like that."

"Then how do you know if it would work?"

"I have blood samples here the coven has collected for my tests."

She nodded. "So, let's assume this works. If I were to take this serum, it would change my blood so you could feed on me and gain the same type of sustenance Olivia feeds her men?"

"Exactly, except it would be closer to a carnivore turning into a vegetarian. Rather than eating meat, they would choose to eat tofu."

She raised her brows. "So, I would theoretically become tofu for you?"

"I would never consider you tofu, but as a purpose of comparison, yes."

She inhaled a long breath, then slowly let it go. "I don't know if I'm ready to take such a leap like this."

"No one is suggesting for you to. It is an option that will be available if you choose to take it. No one would ever ask you to ingest it or force you to do anything you do not wish to do."

"Oh, well that's good to know, but what happens with all of us if I, oh, I don't know, decide to stay with you? If I choose this life but decide to not take the serum. Where does that leave us?"

"It wouldn't be an issue. The coven has volunteers to feed vampires who do not have a blood demon."

"Oh," she whispered. "So, why the serum then?"

"I presented the idea to the coven. If we were able to create a synthetic form of blood for vampires to ingest when blood demons are not an option, it would be a way for us to continue living without the fear of starving. Thus, giving into blood thirst."

"Blood thirst?"

"Yeah, it's not something you ever want to see or experience. For lack of better terms, we basically go mad and lose our mind to the lust of blood. There is no controlling or stopping a vampire who is starved and insane from blood lust."

Fear tinged at the back of her mind. She felt like bait in a pool full of sharks. All it took was a small prick of her blood and the monsters would react. She swallowed hard and sat back in her seat.

"Please, don't worry about any of us. No one would ever put you in danger like that. If any of us were to come close to losing ourselves, we would be removed before any danger would come to you."

"Well, I'm happy to know that." She paused and shifted her gaze to the vial once more. "What would happen to me if I were to take this serum?"

"Nothing physically. You wouldn't feel a thing. Your blood would change to become synthetic. There are some side effects, though."

She raised her brow. "What kind of

side effects?"

"You would not age any further than where you are today. Over time, if the serum worked its way out of your body, the aging process would pick back up, but if you continued to take the serum, you would continue to remain youthful."

"Well, that's not so bad."

He smiled. "You could be two hundred years of age and look no older than you do right now."

"Wow," she whispered. "A part of me says sign me up!" She laughed, then continued. "The other part is still wary of experimenting with something I know nothing about."

"Completely understood. Only when you're ready, you may take the serum."

She stood from her seat. "Thank you for telling me about this. I don't do well with secrets and appreciate it."

"If this is the life you want, there will never be secrets between any of us."

Chayton placed the vial back in the metal holding tray, then turned back to her. "Do you have questions you'd like to ask?"

"I'm sure I will, but right now, no. What I'd like to do is go rest for a while. I feel like my up is down and dark is light. I feel like Alice when she fell down the rabbit hole."

"That's understandable. You've learned a lot the last few days."

She nodded. "Vampires are real and there's a serum that didn't come from the fountain of youth." She paused, meeting his gaze. "Are there shifters in the world, or any other kind of fae?"

He smiled and took a few steps toward her. Reaching for her, he slid a soft, gentle hand across her cheek and - brushed a few strands from her face. "There's so much more for you to learn about our world, but in time, Tawne."

She nodded and tilted her head into

the palm of his hand. "You've been so kind to me, without knowing anything about me."

"We know plenty," he whispered. "You love history and long to become a museum curator, but this is not what makes you. What makes you is your passion, your boldness for life, the fact you were willing to take a leap with a group of men who were not from your world. It speaks a lot about you as a person."

"You make it sound like you're an alien."

He chuckled. "Well, not quite. I do have a question."

She lifted her gaze to his. He was so close. She wanted to reach for him, pull him close, have him hold her the way Cristofano and Evan did. "Sure."

"Since we first met, and more so now that we're alone, I want to kiss you. I want to feel your body against mine. I want to taste every inch of your body and have you experience the most amazing pleasure of your life."

Her breath rushed from her lips and her knees felt weak. She'd felt chilled in this room, but right now, she was hot and needed to remove her clothes. She longed to lie on his metal table while he touched her body. Her face warmed with the blood that rushed to her cheeks. "I would love that."

His brows rose, and he grinned. Chayton tilted her head up and leaned in. He slanted his lips across hers and possessed her body with a friction that demanded dominance. One of his arms wrapped around her body and he held her close against him.

Tawne needed more. Having kissed Cristofano and Evan, and now Chayton, she began to understand what Olivia had been feeling with her men. It was possible to have more than one man in your life, with feelings for all of them. She wanted this, needed this. She moved her hands up his chest and around his neck, pulling him closer.

His hair fell into his face, ticking her cheeks. Chayton pulled back and looked into her eyes. "You're a beautiful woman, Tawne. I want so much more from you, but I'm afraid to ask of it. Go, get your rest. We have plenty of time for this." He rested his forehead against hers and let a sigh fan against her lips.

She nodded. "I should go. I'm concerned if I don't leave, I may end up taking advantage of you."

He chuckled. "I find that very doubtful. I'm more than willing to comply."

She laughed and let him go, taking a few steps back. "I'll find my way back to my room. I think I want to rest on my sundeck."

He grinned. "Do that, please. Tonight, if you'll allow us, we can taste the sun on your skin."

Her brows rose. "Can you really?"

"In a way, yes. As soon as the sun is down, we'll come find you."

"What about Will?"

"He'll either be there or will join us. Either way, he'll be with us."

She bit her bottom lip. "I don't think he cares for me much. What's his story?"

Chayton walked her to the elevator and pressed the button. The doors slid open. He took her inside and pressed the third-floor button. "That's his story to tell when he's ready."

"Okay. Then I'll see you tonight."

He reached for her hand and brought it to his lips. "I look forward to it." He stepped out of the elevator and the doors closed.

Tawne leaned against the wall and sighed with a smile. Exhaustion begun to settle in and she yawned. The possibility of having four...well, three men, in her life was becoming more of a reality. The decision was hers if she chose to accept it. What happened if they decided to not choose her? Would Will put a stop to that? It wasn't something she wanted to consider right now. What she needed was her bed.

The elevator doors opened, and she stepped out. Down the hall she found Will walking toward his room. He stopped just before he stepped inside and turned to look at her.

She stared at him down the length of the hall and offered a smile, then lowered her gaze. She didn't want to deal with him or his personality just before napping. When she glanced back up, he had disappeared into his room.

She shuffled the few steps needed to get to her room and closed the door behind her. Grabbing one of the pillows off her bed, she removed the lab jacket Chayton gave her, her shoes, and clothes. She left her bra and panties on. Feeling a chill, she picked up a light blanket that was folded on the end of her bed.

Opening her balcony door, she stepped out and lifted her face toward the sun. The rays warmed her, and she smiled. Lying down on her chaise, she tucked the pillow under her head and covered her body with the blanket. She closed her eyes and, in her exhaustion, sleep quickly claimed her. Darkness gave way to erotic dreams of three vampires seducing her, with another in the background, closing in.

Chapter Eleven

THE SKIES WERE touched with soft clouds and the air smelled of crisp afternoon sunlight. There was a slight chill in the air and goose bumps scattered across Tawne's skin. She inhaled a deep breath and raised her arms above her head. She stretched and felt renewed from her afternoon nap.

Having spent time with Cristofano, Chayton, and Evan left her with an easy feeling of a school girl falling in love with her high school crush...times three.

She wanted more than a schoolgirl crush, though. She wanted an undying love that would last an eternity and never falter. Wanting the fantasy had never met the needs of reality, though. It was an unfortunate circumstance that comes with being a human woman with emotions.

Here's my baggage, universe. Take it all and let me know how you manage with the weight of it. See you on the flip side!

She sighed at her own inner musings and reached for the side table. Her hand tapped across the marble top, but her fingers found nothing. She opened her eyes and examined the emptiness before her.

Well, this is disappointing.

"Would you like a drink?"

She gasped with a start and sat up in her chair. Turning around, she found Cristofano, Evan, and Chayton watching her. She laughed and placed her hand over her heart. "My gods, you frightened me!" Remembering she was only in her undergarments, she tugged the blanket up to her shoulders.

"My apologies," Cristofano offered with a grin. "It was not the intent."

"How long have you been out here?"

Chayton looked at the other two, then glanced at the watch on his wrist. "Maybe twenty minutes."

She met his gaze with raised brows. "That's kinda stalkerish of you, you know?"

Evan chuckled. "Not really. We picked up on some kind of erotic fantasy you were having in your sleep. We hoped to wait for you to awake from such a stupor and allow us to recreate said dream with you."

She coughed, and her face heated as the blood rushed upward. "You wish to do what?"

Cristofano took a step forward, remaining in the shadows of the balcony. "We wish to offer you what you're clearly longing for. No strings. We only wish to please you and give you the release your body has been wanting."

Her clit appeared to have its own heartbeat when her nether regions warmed with a pleasant throb. She crossed her legs and squeezed them together in an effort to extinguish the fire threatening to give away her repressed sexual desire.

"I... I have no idea what you mean," she whispered.

"Oh, I think you do," Cristofano countered. "Come to us, Tawne. Allow us to give you want you're longing for, what your body needs. Let us give ourselves to you."

She swallowed the dryness in her throat and stood from her seat. She held the blanket around her body for a moment. Her stomach flipped in excitement and in nerves. Lifting her gaze to Cristofano's, she dropped the cover and revealed her near naked body. She took the few steps necessary and positioned herself before Cristofano, Evan, and Chayton.

"I don't know if I'm ready for this," she whispered. "I've never been with more than one man at a time."

Cristofano placed a gentle finger underneath her chin and tilted her head up. "No one will be penetrating you with their cocks today, my love. Today is for you, and you alone. We wish for you to only enjoy what we may be able to offer you."

"No sex?" She questioned.

"Correct," Chayton whispered behind her. He tugged her hair and pulled it to the side. His breath teased her shoulder when he licked across the pulsing vein of her neck.

"Oh god," she whispered and closed her eyes.

Cristofano tilted her head slightly then slipped his tongue across her lips. She opened her mouth for him and he slanted his mouth over hers.

Chayton placed his hands over her waist, then moved them up, over her bra. He cupped her full mounds in his hands, squeezed them, giving her nipples a pinch. "We need to remove this," he whispered and unclasped her bra. He dropped it to the ground and squeezed her bare breasts. Chayton pressed his hips against her ass and Tawne gasped at his erection.

"Turn her to the side. I need to taste her." Evan told them.

She opened her eyes when Evan spoke his desire. The two holding her did as he requested. Cristofano tilted her head toward him and continued to kiss her. Chayton slid his tongue up to her ear and nibbled on her lobe while he massaged her breasts and pinched her nipples.

Evan began at her knees. He kissed her kneecaps, then slipped his hands up the outside of her thighs. He hooked his fingers over the outside of her panties and tugged them over her hips.

Tawne froze. She pulled herself free from Evan, Cristofano, and Chayton. "I... I don't know if I can do this," she whispered in a rushed breath. "I want to, oh gods, do I want to, but this is happening so fast."

"We will leave you be, if that is your wish, Tawne," Cristofano answered. "But, if you allow us, we would love to give ourselves to you."

She bit her bottom lip. If she weren't careful, she might gnaw off her skin. She let the apprehension go and met all three men's stares.

Chayton, Evan, and Cristofano all

stood before her with their dress shirts unbuttoned halfway and sleeves rolled to the elbows. To Tawne, there was nothing sexier than a businessman getting down and dirty in whatever deeds he was about to commit.

Having one man was fun, two felt exciting and naughty. Three men at once... She wanted to call herself a whore, but why? Society standards?

She grinned. Fuck society.

She lifted her chin up and perked a brow. "Come to me," she whispered.

Cristofano smirked and took her left hand. Chayton grasped her right. Both men placed a gentle kiss on the inside of her wrist and made their way to her inner elbows.

Evan on the other hand, he dropped to his knees and reached again for her panties. Giving them another tug, he lowered the garment down her legs, then over her feet.

"Take a seat and lie back," Evan told her. "Relax, my love."

She had never stood naked before a man without the light off. She thought she could do this, but now that she was naked, she wasn't sure. She felt ashamed of her size and a scar on her abdomen. She lowered her gaze and moved her arms to cover her body.

"What are you doing?" Cristofano asked.

She shook her head and felt her eyes burn with tears, then one slipped down and hit her bare breast. "I've never been naked in front of someone with the lights on."

"You are beautiful," Chayton whispered next to her ear. "Please, allow us to see you."

She shook her head. "I can't... I... I'm ugly and fat and scarred."

"You, my love, are a beautiful soul," Cristofano whispered. "We love your curves, your figure, everything. As for the scar," he traced his finger over the side of her stomach. "It's a battle wound to show you can survive in this life. Something tried to claim you, and you fought back. You have a strength in you that I don't think you see."

"Yes, we see it," Evan told her. "We saw it the night we met, and even further witnessed it when you stood up to Will."

She smiled and hiccupped a chuckle. "He kinda deserved that."

"That he did," Cristofano told her. "Now, please, put whatever you're feeling out of your mind. If society is telling you to be thinner, to be taller, to be tanner, shorter, blonde, brown, or purple, society isn't who we want. We want you."

She met his gaze. "Purple?"

He shrugged. "Pink?"

She smiled. "Fuck society." Her thoughts of being with more than one man, and their views on what women should look like, came together in a collision of fuck-all-this-noise and exploded into fireworks of gratitude and longing. She wanted her men and dammit, they wanted her just as much.

Tawne pushed aside any and all feelings of insecurity and sat down on her chaise. She laid back and bent her legs. "Thank you," she whispered.

"You're welcome," Cristofano told her and lowered himself onto his knees. Reaching for her left breast, he gave it a gentle squeeze. He leaned forward and brushed the tip of his tongue over her nipple. The pebbled flesh grew taut to his teasing. He flicked it again with his tongue, and sucked the flesh into his mouth.

She gasped at the sensation his fangs gave when he grazed them over her flesh. It was an erotic feeling mixed with fear, culminating in a sensual seduction. She shifted her gaze to Chayton and found he had lowered himself to his knees. He took the other breast and licked the tip of her nipple and, like Cristofano, he brought the puckered nub to his mouth, teasing it with his tongue and fangs.

A pair of hands rested upon her knees. She looked up at Evan as he sat up, looking down at her form. "Beautiful," he whispered. He placed pressure on her legs and with ease, moved them apart from one another. She opened herself to him and closed her eyes.

"No, my love," he told her. "Open your eyes. Watch me. You are exquisite."

She pressed her lips together and opened her eyes once more. She met his gaze and he offered a smile, which she returned.

"If you wish for me to not do this, I will stop." He pressed his palms to the inside of her thighs and squeezed them, working his way down.

"Don't stop," she answered. "Please."

He nodded and his gaze roved down her body. He focused his attention on her pussy and she could feel herself cream with her two men on both breasts, and the third now lowering himself down on the chaise. He used his hands to push her legs further apart, moving his fingers to trace her labia and come to rest on her clit.

She lifted her head up and gasped when his tongue licked up the length of her, from pussy canal to her clit. She laid her head laid back onto the chair when he did it again. His tongue, gods his majestic tongue, teased her clit with flicks and licks. He sucked on her throbbing nerves, then shoved his tongue inside her channel.

"More," she whispered. "I need more. Use your fingers." She was shocked to hear herself speak the request, but knew it had been heard when Evan slid a finger inside her.

A set of hands slid underneath her head and tilted her neck. She looked up to Cristofano above her. She hadn't realized he'd let go of her breast.

"Are you enjoying yourself now, my love?"

She nodded. "Oh gods, yes." Her body bucked, and a moan escaped her lips, interrupting the silence of her balcony.

He leaned down and tilting her head once more, slanted his lips across hers.

She moaned into his mouth when Evan's finger turned up and made a 'come here' motion against the sensitive spot inside her channel. He sucked on her clit and flicked it with tongue. He pushed in another finger and the motion became harder, faster.

She gasped against Cristofano's mouth. A finger pressed against the puckered hole of her butt and pressed gently. When she opened her eyes, she realized it was Chayton working his finger against her back entrance.

Cristofano laid her head back down and pressed a gentle kiss on her forehead. "Does it hurt with his finger?"

She shook her head no. "I've never experienced anything back there before but there's no pain."

"Do you want more?" Chayton asked her and licked her nipple.

"I'm scared to ask for more. What if I can't stop?"

"We'll make sure to not send you down the rabbit hole too far the first time," Chayton answered. He pulled his hand away from her passage and coated the digits in slick, shiny lube.

She raised her brow. "You had lube with you?"

He shrugged. "Never know when one might need it."

She grinned and closed her eyes.

Hands slid underneath her head and cradled her neck. Lips slipped across hers and Cristofano opened her mouth with this tongue. He teased her tongue and lips just as Chayton slipped a digit back into her hole. He applied pressure and pushed his second finger inside her, all while Evan continued to finger fuck her and suck on her clit.

Chayton pumped his fingers inside her, working a rhythm with the lube. Evan's mouth sucked on her pussy and his fingers pushed in harder and faster. Warmth creamed from her channel and the more he pushed, the stronger it grew. She could hear her core slosh as if she were drenched. In a way, she was.

"Will you come for us?"

She looked up at Cristofano and her lips parted. She nodded and her back arched. "Yes," she told him. "Oh gods, yes!"

Chayton pumped his fingers harder, then spread them inside her in a scissor shape. Then all at once, her body exploded into an orgasm unlike any she had ever experienced in her life. Her back arched and her nipples hardened to sharp peaks.

A rush of heat pushed from her body as Evan continued to thrust his fingers and suck on her clit.

"Oh hell, oh my god, yes! Fuck me," She screamed. "Oh my god, yes!" Her hips bucked and Cristofano cradled her neck. He feathered his lips over hers as she gasped.

"Grab her legs," Evan growled when he raised himself up. Cristofano captured her legs by the back of her knees and pulled them to her chest, then spread them wide.

Evan pushed her pussy lips apart and pressed his index and middle finger against her clit. He moved it back and forth in quick movements, drawing out her orgasm.

Chayton pumped his fingers harder

into her ass. "You love this, don't you?" he whispered.

"Yes!" Tawne screamed her answer and her body shook harder. Another orgasm was building, and she growled in response to it. "Fuck my ass! I'm coming, holy shit, I'm going to fucking come!"

Evan growled and pinched her clit, then captured her pussy with his mouth once more.

Chayton moved his fingers faster. "Imagine my cock inside you."

"Fuck, yes," she groaned. "I need you, all of you, fuck!"

"May I taste you?" The words from Cristofano whispered into her ear and she nodded.

"Yes, please. Do it."

His tongue slipped across her neck. She wasn't sure what happened, but just when he licked her flesh, her body erupted into mass hysteria. Her pussy erupted again, but this time, it was like a faucet had turned on. She came and came hard, drenching her chaise, Chayton's hand, and Evan's face.

Evan growled against her and lapped at her honey. "She tastes like the sweetest wine on my tongue."

Cristofano moaned against her neck and it was then she realized he was sucking on her neck. When he released her, he licked her neck once more, and the sensation rushing through her body subsided. He leaned in and pressed his lips to hers. She tasted blood on his tongue. It was like tasting herself on a man's mouth after he had been down on her. Rather than tasting pussy, she tasted blood, and it was the most delicate sensation she had experienced. It was like tasting a sweet wine followed by the richest tasting chocolate of her life.

Chayton pulled his fingers from her. "Tilt her head toward me, brother." Cristofano obliged and moved her head toward him. He slanted his lips across hers and teased her tongue with his. "Mmm, I can taste you. I cannot wait to sample you for myself."

She smiled. As much as this should scare her, it didn't. "I would love to say do it now, but I think I'm tapped out for a bit."

He chuckled. "I wouldn't right now. But later," he winked with a pause. "We'll give you time to recover."

Evan sat up and ran his hand down his face. "You two have to taste her later. My apologies on not wanting to share, but she has an exquisite taste just right for us." He met her gaze and leaned over her. "I can't wait to taste you again later."

She grinned and allowed her body to lie limp on the chaise. "I need a shower and another nap."

The men chuckled and Tawne squealed when Chayton scooped her into his arms. He carried her inside and walked toward her bathroom. "Your bath awaits, my love."

She leaned into his embrace and closed her eyes. She had never experienced an intense orgasm like she had today, even while using toys. She was curious what sex would be like with them, and she also wondered if Will would be part of her next step.

Chapter Twelve

TAWNE RESTED HER head against the Victorian style bathtub, her arms resting on either side. Her men had drawn her a bubble bath and Chayton had lowered her into the sudsy hot water. It smelled of lavender and vanilla.

She looked around her Parisian embellished bathroom. From the light colors of the stone tile to the cream-colored walls with accents of black and red throughout, this room had to be her favorite out of the entire house. She glanced over at the separate shower. It was large enough to hold at least three people.

I could live in this bathroom and be content.

Art decorated the walls with black and white painted images of couples in downtown Paris. Each portrait featured a red umbrella. On the ceiling hung a chandelier and the crystal lights projected multi-colored beams that danced around the room.

Tawne reflected on her time with Cristofano, Evan, and Chayton. The men lavished her earlier and asked for nothing in return. Would this be her life? Would they continue to be there for her, be anything for her? That's what was promised and so far, they'd held up their end of the promise.

What about next year, the next decade, hell, the next century? Would they grow tired of her? Would Chayton's serum really do what he was suspecting? Would she really be able to live out her life with her men and never age?

Her stomach quivered and felt heavy at the thought of jumping in feet first, then realizing, after the fact, she'd rushed in haste. At this point, only time would tell. Was she ready to commit to this type of lifestyle? If she chose this life, there would be no children or grandchildren, no schools, no PTA planning, nothing. Not that her parents did PTA planning when they were alive, but was this something she may want to consider if she did have children?

What if I want to have a child? Could I? Can they do that?

She sighed and lowered herself further into the tub until she was submerged completely. She imagined her men walking in on her bath time and her looking like a soapy, drowned rat. The thought amused her. Coming up for air, she drained the tub and decided it was time to clean up and see if she could spend some time with the devil...and in this case, the sexy-as-sin and mean as hell, Will.

***

Tawne stood in the hallway outside her bedroom and stared down the corridor where she last saw Will. His room was just down the way, last room on the left. She walked, one foot in front of the other and all the while she wanted to flee. She flexed her fingers, curling and uncurling the digits. If she were to go into this arrangement with these men, it would include Will. She was certain she could do this without him, but she would never ask the others to not include him. It wouldn't be fair. Like a lineup of picking teams and being the last one. The team would be obligated to take him. The situations were different, but the feelings of being last were the same. The hurt would be real and, regardless how much they may end up hating one another, she would never put that much hurt into someone's heart.

She had been that person in the past, the one picked last. She was never good at sports, at debate, and most of all, standing up for herself. That changed, though, when her parents passed away. She had no one left in her family, except Olivia. Her best friend had become the sister she never had. If it weren't for her, she wasn't sure she would have made it this far.

She sighed when she finally stood in front of Will's door. She recalled the times when Olivia told her to stand up for herself, that if she refused, who would fight for her?

'Fight for what you want, and never back down. Fight for it! If you stand for nothing, you'll fall for anything.'

"Didn't someone famous say that last part?" Tawne had asked.

She smiled to herself as she recalled their conversation. *She's right. I need to fight for what I want and, dammit, I want this. I need this in my life.*

A part of her wondered if she wanted this because she was alone and felt desperate. The other part felt as if something inside her she didn't know was dormant had been awakened. She didn't want to lose that feeling.

She would fight.

Tawne raised her fist and closed her eyes, then knocked on the door.

"What do you want, Tawne?"

She opened her eyes. The door had not opened, but Will knew she was outside. Of course he did. He's a vampire and could sense feelings, or something. Like the others. Yet, he wanted to know what she wanted?

"I don't know." She looked down at the

clothes she'd opted for this moment. In her closet were more clothes than she knew what to do with, but for this occasion, she picked a pastel yellow, halter style sundress with a white shrug and white sandals.

She continued and stared at the door. "Since you know it's me, tell me what I want." She cringed as soon as the words were out of her mouth. So often, words spewed from her before she had a chance to think about what she wanted to say.

The door unlatched and was pulled open with a hard thrust, and an angry Will stood on the other side. He frowned and furrowed his brows.

She met the dark brown evil stare of his eyes and took a step back. His tight fitted white tank top compressed and released over his pectorals. His arms were bare, and the muscles tensed and released with each movement he made.

He took a step forward and his lip

curled in what could only be described as disgust. "I said, what the hell do you want?"

She frowned, and her stomach fell into her shoes. Her body trembled, and she opened her mouth to speak, but only squawked. Her heart raced in her chest and she took a step back.

"No, don't you leave now. You've got my fucking attention. Tell me what you want!"

She let go of the breath she'd been holding and squared her shoulders. The fear started to drain and was replaced by anger—no rage. Heat rushed up her neck and her face and ears grew hotter. She fisted her hands and her arms shook for a different reason.

"What the fuck is your problem with me?" she yelled.

His brows rose, and his mouth opened agape. He blinked a few times, then frowned once more. "Fuck off." He turned his back on her and started to shut the door. "I would never want you."

She gasped and put her foot by the door and held it open with her hands. "You could never have me!"

He whirled on her and grabbed her by the shoulders. He yanked her inside, slamming the door behind her. "You're a human piece of shit. Do you need me to go on?"

Tawne screamed and dug her nails into her palms. Her throat stung from it, but she also felt a huge release of adrenaline. She took a few steps toward him and it surprised her to see Will stepping backward. "You're a piece of shit dead man who doesn't deserve me or to be happy!" She pointed her finger at him and continued. "I don't know who the fuck took a shit in your bowl of I-hate-everyone-Cheerios, but it wasn't me and you don't get to treat me this way!" She continued her verbal assault until they stopped, and Will was pressed against a wall. She stepped into his space and poked his chest. "What the hell is your problem?"

"You're human is my problem!"

She flinched at his words and lowered her hand. "You were human once. Why is it an issue with me being human?"

Will sagged at against the wall, as if he had given up on their fight. He lifted a brow. "You won't stop or leave until I tell you, am I right?"

She shrugged. "I would never ask anyone to divulge anything they're not comfortable to tell, but in this case, I deserve to know why you hate me without even knowing me."

"You're tougher than you look, you know that?"

She took another step back. "I have no one else to stand up for me or defend me."

He sidestepped her and made his way

across the room to his desk. It was then she took a moment to look around his bedroom. It was kept neat. Bed made, a few art pieces on the wall, and law books on bookshelves. It was a large room, like hers, but it didn't have a balcony.

He stood next to a wall that had a dark mahogany armoire with a set of double doors and a large drawer below it. Will opened the doors and inside were four crystal carafes. Three contained a brown liquid except one, it was clear. Water maybe?

He lifted two crystal brandy glasses and poured one brown liquid into them. He turned and made his way back to Tawne, then handed her a glass.

"It's whiskey. I figured we'd start here."

She nodded and accepted the glass. "Thank you."

He lifted the contents then drained the glass.

She raised her brows. "Does the

whiskey have any effect on you?"

"None whatsoever."

"Then why drink it?"

He sat his glass down and walked over to his desk in the room. He took a seat pressed a button on his laptop. The screen came to life and she looked to see what he had been working on.

"The whiskey reminds me of my life as a human. I used to enjoy it."

She took a few steps toward him. He motioned to another chair by the desk. She pulled it out and took a seat, then sipped her whiskey.

"Is that music sheets?"

He nodded. "Yes."

She looked to him and raised her brows again. "You write music?"

"Yes. I also play."

"The piano and cello, those are yours?"

He nodded again. "Yes."

"Wow, I never would have thought you played."

"I'm quite good."

She took another sip. "I have no doubt."

A moment of silence passed between them. Tawne thought to say something else, but this was Will's story to tell. She wasn't sure what she was about to hear or experience, but she wanted to give him time. She knew it had taken her a long time to talk about her parents death, but this was his pain, not hers.

"Can I tell you something?" she asked.

"I have a feeling you will regardless of what I say."

A small laugh sounded in the room and Tawne smiled. "You have me figured out already."

Will perked a crooked smile at her remark.

"My parents died a few years ago in a horrific car accident."

He met her gaze and held it for a moment. "I'm very sorry."

"I am, too. It hurt me for a long time and I couldn't talk about it. I didn't want to. But, not talking tore me up inside. I felt myself becoming bitter."

"You realize I'm not you, right?"

She nodded. "I'm only trying to help."

He moved the mouse across the screen and pressed the save button. With a sigh, he sat back in his chair and crossed his arms over his chest. "I'm surprised the others didn't tell you."

Tawne sipped her whiskey. "It's not their story to tell."

Will let his head relax back on his seat and stared at the ceiling. He had facial hair cut close to the skin. A part of her wanted to rub her palms on the scruff, the other was frightened he may try to bite her if she did.

"I was born and raised in California. I grew up in a home built on dirt that had a leaky roof. My father was an abusive drunk. When I was five, my mother left us and I never saw her again. I had no brothers or sisters. It was just me and my father." He paused for a moment in reflection of his memories.

Tawne wanted to reach out and take his hand, squeeze it, let him know she was there, but she remained in her seat instead.

"Women came and went week after week. One of them stayed longer than the others. Her name was Holly."

When he spoke Holly's name, there was a hollowness to it. Pain came with her name and Tawne was about to hear something she may regret later in asking.

"Holly took it upon herself to teach me all about sexual education. I was twelve years old."

"Oh god, Will, I'm so sorry."

He tilted his head toward Tawne. "There's a lot more. Are you sure you want to hear this?"

She sat her glass down and scooted

her chair closer. "Will, I had no idea. You don't have to tell me this."

He turned his head up and stared at the ceiling. "She sexually molested me a few times a week. When I turned thirteen, she took it further. She decided she would train me to become a Dom, but in order to do that she forced me to submit to her. I tried to tell my father what she was doing, but he only backhanded me and told me I was lying.

"One night, when Holly was higher than a fucking cloud, she came into my room. I think I was already fifteen, maybe sixteen by then. She came in there and crawled into my bed, on top of me. I'd had enough of her and my father. Something inside me snapped.

"I fought back against Holly and knocked her out. I honestly thought I had killed her. I grabbed a few things of mine and ran away."

He paused in his story and stood from

his chair. Will checked his watch then walked over to the windows of his room. He pulled the curtains open and the light of the moon illuminated the dark sky.

"Eventually, I wound up in a foster home. The abuse didn't stop there. It became physical. If anything, the beatings taught me how to fight. I held my own against the man of the house a few times, but when I turned eighteen, I was kicked out.

"I lived between homes on people's beds, back porches, bars, or the forested area. Anywhere I could get work or somewhere to get food or water, I took it. I resorted to stealing clothes a few times when mine were outgrown or were ripped.

"On my twenty-fifth birthday, I went down to Hollywood in hope of finding work, or you know, getting discovered. The movie, *The Cabinet of Dr. Caligari*, had released a few years prior and horror was the way to go it seemed. *Doctor Jekyll and Mister Hyde* were quite popular, as they still are today.

"My goal was clear. I needed a positive change and the only way to do it was with money. Hollywood had it and I wanted it. I was hired by a local film company to clean the sets, work on building things, stuff like that. I worked during the days since the movies were mainly shot at night. I seldom saw my employer, but when I did, it was quick moments. He was there, then he wasn't. It was very odd. I grew curious about what went on during the filming sessions. So, one night, I decided to stay. I hid in one of the backdrop areas.

"What came next, it changed everything I ever knew about our world."

Tawne's grip tightened in her lap. She fisted her hands in anticipation of what would be coming next. He had already been through so much.

"Women were brought into the set to audition for roles...or so I thought. They began to read the lines and the men surrounded them acting out their parts. Then, when the women were not expecting it, the men attacked them. They bit into their necks and blood spewed in all different directions."

"Holy shit," she whispered.

He turned and met her gaze. "I screamed, and they found me."

"What happened?" She knew what happened. The end result stood before her.

"They found me and brought me out into the open. I was bound to a seat and forced to watch the brutal rape, feeding on, and murder of the women."

"Oh, Will," she whispered.

"I saw the worst of humanity that night, but for me, it still wasn't over."

Tawne wiped away a tear that slipped down her cheek. Her heart bled for the man before her. Everything became clear—his hatred for humans, why he didn't want her there, everything.

"When they were done with the women, the leader, the man who hired me, took my life. He bit into me, then forced his blood down my throat. He changed me that night, then left me for dead. My body was dumped into an alley." He turned back to the window and looked out upon the night sky once more.

"Malik found me soon after I was turned. He brought me back to New Orleans and took me into his family. He gave me everything I never had. He encouraged me to go to school and earn a degree in something, to create a career for myself. It would keep me busy, I suppose. I decided to go into law to protect those who could not protect themselves."

Tawne stood from her chair and crossed the room to where Will stood. He had his hands in his pockets and didn't move when she approached. She laid her hands on the back of his shoulders. He didn't move away from her this time. She took this as a positive thing.

"I am so sorry," she whispered. "I didn't know, any of it."

"There's nothing to apologize for, Tawne. It wasn't you."

"No, it wasn't, but I understand the hatred for humans. You knew nothing but hate, torture, and demise." She paused and rested her forehead against the middle of his back. She felt his muscles move but remained where she was. "I promise, I'm not like any of those monsters. I promise to never hurt you like that, or anyone in my life."

"Tawne," he whispered and turned to face her.

She took a step back and looked up into his eyes. "Yes?"

"Thank you for listening. My brothers

here know, and Malik, but no one else."

"It stays with me and me alone. I promise you."

He nodded. "Thank you."

"You're welcome. Thank you for sharing."

He touched her cheek with the back of his hand, then leaned in. "I'm sorry for holding you accountable for what my past did. It wasn't fair."

"Thank you," she whispered. "May I kiss you?"

He didn't have to answer. He leaned in and his lips captured hers in a kiss of desperation. He cradled her head with both hands and leaned into her, tipping her back.

She gripped his forearms and held on. His tongue danced with hers in a power struggle of dominance. She gasped, and her head tilted back when his mouth pressed against her neck.

"We must stop," he growled against

her throat, "or I will not be able to control myself around you."

She longed to have this man on top of her, inside, her, claiming her, along with the other three. Her heart raced as she pulled herself free from his grip. "I want you to lose control. I want you to claim me with the others. I want to be yours."

He tilted her face to his and stared into her eyes, directly into her soul. "Are you sure this is what you want?

"Yes," she whispered. "I want you, all of you."

A knock rapped on the door. Tawne took a step back from Will, and lowered her gaze to the floor.

"What's wrong?" Will asked.

The universe saying wait?

She shook her head, then looked at him with a smile. "Nothing. This morning I wasn't sure what would be in store for me...for us. All of us. I'll be honest with you, though. Everything that's happened today? I never expected any of it."

He touched her underneath her chin and lifted her head up. Will leaned in and pressed his lips to her forehead. "Sometimes we need someone to remind us of our humanity."

She closed her eyes. His words... No one had given her a compliment as deep, as meaningful, as Will's. It took her to a new place within herself, a place she didn't know existed until she met her men. There was a side to Tawne that had been dormant for far too long. Her men summoned this part of her she didn't know existed and brought out a beast within.

She followed Will with her eyes as he crossed the room to his bedroom door. He turned the knob and peeked around the doorjamb, then stepped back and fully opened it. On the other side were Cristofano, Evan, and Chayton.

The three joined the fourth and

together the quartet became the predators. Tawne was their prey and a fire ignited between her legs, an intense longing for the four of them to devour her, claim her, and give themselves to only her burned itself deep inside her very soul.

Chapter Thirteen

TAWNE MET THE gaze of her men, staring into each of their eyes, each of their souls. Her body trembled with anticipation, but also with fear. Having never been with more than one man at a time was new territory for her. Earlier in the day, when the trio seduced her on the balcony, it was almost too much to encounter. She opened herself to her men fully, freely.

However, now there were four, and if sex were to happen, and she wanted it as much as she did earlier, if not more, she was ready. She nibbled on her lip and perked a grin from the corner of her mouth.

"How did we get so lucky to have a woman such as Tawne?" Cristofano asked the group.

"I don't know. It helps knowing people," Evan offered. "If it weren't for Olivia, we may never have met our woman."

Our woman. The words repeated in Tawne's mind. They were closing in around her in four corners: north, south, east, and west. Each were within an arm's reach, but no one had ventured to touch her, at least not yet. They were eyeing her up and down, as if measuring the resilience of a prize before it was opened to see what might lie inside.

Watch out boys, there's a beast waiting to pounce.

"Imagine how she'll taste once the

serum is in her body," Chayton said. "She will be sweet on the tongue now, but later, she will be a divine essence we can no longer live without."

Will stood before her, the north point of her quartet. He took a step forward and cupped her face in his hands. "I'm tired of waiting," he whispered and slanted his lips across hers.

A jolt of fire rushed through her body and a moan escaped her throat with a gasp. Her heart raced in her chest and her knees buckled at the intensity of his assault on her lips.

Will scooped her up into his arms. He pulled back and held her gaze for a moment. "You are as sweet as the finest wine."

"It is good to see you two managed to talk," Cristofano said.

"Yes," Will said and held onto her gaze. "She has a way with words herself." He grinned and made his way over to his bed. He sat her down, then stood next to her, along with her three other men.

She met each of their gazes. Each one of them shone with desire and longing.

Cristofano loosened his tie and removed it, followed by unbuttoning his shirt. Evan and Chayton did the same, except Will. Rather than undressing himself, he bent down at Tawne's feet.

Reaching for her legs, he slipped his hand behind her right knee. His touch slipped down the length of her leg to her ankle. He removed her sandal, then did the same to the other leg.

"Are you ready for this?" Will asked her and met her gaze.

A shallow breath escaped when she whispered, "Yes."

He stood and held a hand out for her. She took it and he pulled her to her feet. He took the shrug and slipped it down her arms, then tossed it to the floor.

"Can we take a moment to appreciate

the beauty of this woman?" Will announced.

The four men stood around her in a semi-circle. Cristofano finished unbuttoning his shirt and slid it from his shoulders, letting it fall to the floor. The man was chiseled with strong pectorals, abs, and this V-shaped muscle that disappeared underneath his pants.

Evan tossed his shirt and unbuttoned his pants, letting them fall to the floor. He stood before her with what could only be defined as a beautiful erection. Pressed against his fitted boxer briefs, his manhood strained to remain confined. She had a sudden urge to fall to her knees and take him fully in her mouth.

Before she had a chance to do it, the men groaned, and their heads lolled back in unison, and eyes closed.

She raised her brows. "What happened?" *Did they just get off on something that hasn't happened yet?*

"Whatever you're thinking just shot through each of us," Chayton answered. "It was something erotic in nature and each of us felt it."

"Oh hell," she whispered. "Well, then it's a good thing you can't read minds."

"No," Will grunted, "but we can pick up on your thoughts just as clearly."

She smirked.

Will removed his shirt and tossed it behind him, then unbuttoned his pants. Unlike Evan, Will wore no underwear. His cock was hard, and a bead of anticipation formed on the head.

She licked her lips and looked up into his eyes.

He lifted a brow and one corner of his mouth lifted in a grin. Will had a dark line of hair that led from his chest to his naval, then nothing below that. Did the man wax down there? It didn't matter to her. She wanted to suck on his balls and stroke his cock.

"Fuck, woman," he groaned.

She reached behind her neck and untied her dress. Tawne shifted her gaze to Chayton. She let her dress fall over her breasts and her nipples grew taut from the chill in the air, as well as the anticipation of her men sucking hard on her. She pressed her thighs together in an effort to not cream down the inside of her thighs. Pushing her dress down her body, she stepped out of it and stood in only her white lacy panties.

Chayton removed his shirt and his tanned body was sculpted as if he were the masterpiece of an artist. His chest flexed, as did his arms. She salivated with need, wanting to memorize each of them with her hands, her tongue...every part of herself. It was then she noticed three of her four men trimmed their chest hairs close to their bodies and as it grew narrow down the torso until it reached their naval. She stepped toward Chayton and laid her palms upon his bare chest. Unlike his brothers, he did not have body hair. Maybe this was a Native American thing, but she didn't mind.

She slid her palms up his body, over his nipples, around his neck. She pressed her naked body against his.

"Well, hello there, beautiful," he whispered.

She smiled and pulled him down toward her. Chayton tilted his head and licked her lips in a tease before he curved his mouth over hers. He cupped her ass and squeezed her, pulling her pelvis against the hard manhood pressing against her body. She wanted to wrap her legs around his body and feel his cock slide up and down against her folds, teasing her clit and making her cream on his balls.

Another set of hands touched the back

of her legs and slid upward over her hips. Fingers gathered into the edge of her panties and tugged. The fabric slid down her legs and she stepped out of them.

Chayton moved his hands to her waist and a body pressed up against her backside. Lips feathered across her shoulder and her hair was tugged to the side. A naked cock pressed against her ass and silent excitement rushed up her spine. A quick turn of her head revealed it was Will. He pressed his cock against the slit of her ass and moved his pelvis up and down. She wanted to bend over and give herself to him.

Chayton dropped down to his knees. He lifted one of her legs up and over his shoulder, then with gentle fingers, he pushed the labia covering her clit to the sides.

"Damn, woman," he whispered. "You're so wet." He leaned in and teased her with a flick of his tongue.

Tawne gasped and a whine escaped from her. She needed more, so much more. She wanted him to bury his face into her pussy and lick, suck, and swallow every drop of her orgasm. However, giving her a teasing flick once or twice would not bring her to orgasm.

"More," she cried. "Please, more."

He lifted his gaze to hers and arched a brow. "Are you begging?"

She nodded. "Yes, I'm not above begging for my pussy to be eaten."

He smirked then looked past her to Will. "Do you hear that, brother? She's not above begging."

"That I did," Will whispered next to her ear. "Tell him how bad you want it. Tell him you need to come."

"Please," she pleaded once more. "Please, I need to come, please. Stop teasing me."

Chayton pressed his thumb to her clit and moved back and forth in slow, deliberate strokes. "I want to bury my dick deep inside you while Will takes you from behind. What do you think about that?"

She gasped, and leaned her head back until it rested on Will's shoulder. She closed her eyes and could picture Chayton penetrating her pussy while Will claimed her ass.

"Tawne," Cristofano called to her.

She tilted her head to the left and gazed at the man sitting in an armless chair. He sat naked and stroked his thick cock. Using his other hand, he motioned for her to come to him.

Chayton pressed his mouth against her pussy and kissed her clit, then slicked his tongue over it, giving her nub a sharp flick. He lowered her leg and sat back on his heels.

She took a few steps toward Cristofano and her thighs slicked together with each step. She stood over him and stared down at his engorged manhood in his grasp. She wanted to stroke him with her hands, take him into her mouth, give him what they wanted to offer her. She lowered herself to her knees.

Cristofano kept his hand gripped on his cock and tilted the head toward her mouth.

She licked the pearl drop on the head of his shaft.

He grunted and pressed his dick to her lips, smearing the precum across her mouth.

"Take it," he growled.

And she did. Tawne opened her mouth and lowered herself onto his cock, taking him in until his head touched the back of her throat. She formed a suction around his shaft and pulled back until her lips reached the helmet of his manhood.

"Fuck, yes," he groaned. "Suck it, baby."

Fingers teased her pussy from behind

and two thick digits pushed inside her. Tawne moved her legs apart further. Fingers pressed against her clit and teased it by moving back and forth while the other fingers pumped vigorously into her pussy.

She moaned around the cock in her mouth while she sucked and swallowed his head.

"Someone take her from the back and claim that ass," Cristofano ordered.

The words should have frightened her. She had never had anal sex before, but in this moment, she wanted someone to fuck her ass, and pussy, at the same time. She pushed back with a moan against the fingers fucking her core and teasing her clit.

"See? She wants it as much as we do," Will announced.

Warmth poured down her ass cheeks and over her puckered hole. A finger teased her rim and smothered the lube around the entrance, then pushed inside.

Her nipples hardened, and she gasped around the cock in her mouth. The finger pushed in further then pulled back and pushed again. Another set of hands grabbed her ass and pulled her cheeks apart. More lube was poured over her and another finger pushed inside her hole, stretching the tight ring of muscle to the point of edging on a delicious burning pain.

She groaned and pushed back onto the fingers penetrating her ass and pussy. The ones in her channel went from teasing to a vigorous thrust. The sound grew louder with each plunge into her core, drawing more honey from her with the assault.

Another finger pushed inside her ass. The digits scissored inside her, stretching her muscles beyond the point she'd ever thought possible.

She pulled up on Cristofano's cock,

the suction growing tighter the closer to the tip she came, until a pop sounded, and she released him.

"Fuck, woman," he groaned.

"I need someone inside me. Now," she announced. "Please," she groaned. She looked behind her and found it was Will's fingers inside her ass, and Evan's inside her pussy. She looked up at Evan who stood next to the chair. Pressing her palms against Cristofano's knees, she lifted herself up. "Come, fuck my mouth," she told Evan.

Evan reached for her and grabbed a handful of her hair, yanking her head back.

She gasped and opened her mouth for him.

He pushed his cock into her mouth and began to thrust, fucking her mouth. The head hit the back of her throat and he pushed in further, holding himself there until she gagged. He pulled out and allowed her to breathe, then did it again.

"Let's move to the floor. I need to fuck this pussy," Chayton said.

Evan held his cock in her mouth for a moment. When she gagged, he reached for the drool that slipped down her chin. He pulled his dick out and smeared the captured spit onto his cock. "Go," he told her. "Let him fuck you."

Tawne shifted her gaze to Chayton who now lay on the floor, stroking his cock. She smirked and looked at Will behind her.

He removed his fingers from her ass and the grin that spread across his lips read sinister. She couldn't wait to feel him in her ass.

Moving across the floor like a panther stalking their prey, she straddled Chayton's body and moved her hips up and down his body. His cock worked against her like friction, rubbing her clit and pussy. She could orgasm now, just by rubbing herself against his manhood.

He hadn't penetrated her yet, but once she leaned forward, it would all begin. A shudder rushed up her spine as the anticipation skyrocketed. She needed him, all of them, in her, on her, surrounding her.

She leaned forward, ready for her men to claim her. "Fuck me," she whispered and slanted her mouth against Chayton's.

She felt his arm reach between them and line his dick up to her entrance, and push. He slid deep inside her channel, stretching her walls around his cock. He thrust his hips up against her, drawing out a moan with each plunge.

Evan sat down on his knees to her left, then Cristofano to her right. Both men stroked their cocks next to her face. She turned to Evan and opened her mouth. He fisted his hand in her hair and drove his manhood into the back of her throat.

Warmth oozed down her ass once more and a thumb smeared it around her rim. Will was behind her and her body shuddered again with the anticipation of him fucking her ass.

The head of Will's cock pressed against her puckered hole and penetrated the entrance. "Relax, baby," he told her in a gentle, soothing voice. "I don't want to hurt you."

The head of his cock pushed into her and he paused for a moment, allowing her muscles to relax around the invasion of his manhood. Then he pushed further. Slowly, his cock pushed inside her until he was buried in her ass to his balls. Will pulled back and pushed in with small, gentle thrusts.

"Does this hurt?" he asked.

She groaned around the cock in her mouth.

"I think she's good," Cristofano answered for her.

She groaned louder, as if confirming what her lover had announced.

Will pulled back, then with a more aggressive thrust, plunged his cock into her ass.

Tawne yelled out and Evan removed his cock from her mouth. She panted and felt as if her body had just exploded into one massive orgasm. The moment Will pounded her ass just that one time, her pussy broke like a dam.

"Fuck, her pussy is drenched. She's orgasmed hard," Chayton announced. "Fuck her harder."

"Gladly," Will said and thrust his dick harder into her ass. He picked up momentum, plunging into her harder and harder as below her Chayton did the same. The men worked in rhythm. As one pushed, the other pulled.

Tawne lost herself to her men. Her thighs were slick with her honey and her orgasm kept rushing through her body like an unending well. With each thrust in her ass, she screamed in a frenzy and her body spasmed and bucked.

And she still needed more. She had only experienced Chayton and Will. She wanted Evan and Cristofano.

As if picking up on her thoughts, Will gripped her hips and thrust into her harder and faster.

She screamed, and her head tilted back.

Chayton pulled free from her pussy. He cupped her breasts in his hands and pushed them together, then licked the taut nipples, nipping them with his fangs.

Will did not let up on his assault. He growled, and the sound should have frightened her, but it only heightened the sensation he was giving her.

Chayton licked around her left nipple, then his fangs penetrated her skin. She became unglued from every aspect of her being. His fangs biting into her body felt as if he injected her with a substance that allowed her to feel everything she did, but with the feelings intensified by ten...no, twenty.

Will slowed his thrusts and came to a stop. He pulled his cock from her ass and bent over her body. He licked the back of her shoulder and, like Chayton, he buried his fangs in her skin.

Her pussy seeped more of her orgasm down the inside of her thighs.

"I need someone inside me, please," she begged. "I need you, all of you."

"Bring her to me," Cristofano ordered. Chayton released her and licked where he'd bit her, and Will did the same.

Helping her to her feet, Evan touched her under the chin and lifted her face up. "Are you okay?"

She smiled and nodded. "I am amazing and far from done."

"That's my girl," he told her.

"I want to fuck your ass," Cristofano told her. "Now, come here, woman."

She smirked and turned her back to him.

"I'll guide you down. Just spread your legs and I'll do the rest."

She nodded and did as he requested. She felt his hands on her hips as he moved her back and downward. His cock pressed against her hole and he paused for a single heartbeat before he pushed his cock inside her and she slid down his hard shaft, completely engulfing him.

He reached for her legs and pulled them apart, holding them wide, opening her core to the men in front of her.

Cristofano plunged his cock deep, thrusting hard into her ass as he gripped her legs hard against her body.

"Holy fuck," she screamed. Her pussy exploded with another orgasm.

"Fuck yeah," she heard Evan announce. "She's squirting."

Any other time, the words, *she's squirting*, would have had her running for the hills. In this moment, though, she wanted to squirt again, preferably on their faces and cocks.

"Who's going to fuck or eat her pussy?" Cristofano asked.

"Me," Evan answered. He lowered himself to his knees and buried his face against her wide open pussy, licking her clit, swallowing her orgasm, and shoving his fingers inside her channel. "Fuck, yes," he groaned against her slick core.

Behind her, Cristofano licked her neck and bit into her flesh. She screamed out when another orgasm ripped through her.

She glanced down at Evan when he came up and swiped at his mouth with a grin. He leaned in once more and licked the inside of her thigh, then sank his razor sharp teeth into her leg.

Chayton took her left arm and Will her

right. Both men licked the surface of her skin, then bit into her.

Tawne closed her eyes and gave herself over to her men. She was theirs and they were hers. She could never go back to what was now that she'd had a small sampling of her future. Desire and lust held nothing over what she was experiencing.

All at once, the men released their bites on her body. One by one, they licked the puncture wounds and her skin healed over, leaving nothing but faint red marks. Evan stood and leaned over her body, then pushed his cock inside her pussy.

"Oh my god," she screamed and rested her head back on Cristofano. If she were to submit everything she was, everything she knew to her men, this would become her life. She would give up all things of her world to step into theirs. In this moment, she would be willing to do just that.

Chapter Fourteen

LIVING A LIFE of darkness, never seeing the world for what it truly was, had to be worse than death. Beauty, desire, happiness, and heartbreak, all of the human emotions were feelings death would never experience. However, if the blinders of darkness were lifted, and the light the new world fell onto the being for the first time, anything and everything became a possibility.

Tawne had lived in this darkness her entire life. When Olivia brought her into this new world, the shadow that sheltered her life lifted. She viewed the world with new eyes and a sense of self for the first time, the light warmed her skin, it enveloped her body with comfort, and it was also frightening.

The new light in her life had four names: Cristofano, Evan, Chayton, and Will.

Cristofano warmed her sense of self. Being near him cloaked her with an invisible shield. Being with him, she felt safe, wanted, nurtured. She would want for nothing so long as he was by her side.

Evan comforted her, like wrapping a favorite blanket around yourself, loving the smell, the touch of the fabric, everything. He was home for Tawne.

Chayton elated her with wonder, laughter, and contentment. With Chayton, she would always smile, learn something new, bounce ideas off of him with no fear of judgment. He would possess her in a way that allowed her to let go, lose herself to the moment, fly without fear of falling.

Then there was Will. He frightened her above anything else, but it wasn't fear of him, it was fear of herself. She feared ever allowing someone to know her, the real her, to allow that vulnerability to be taken advantage of. With Will, every bit of herself was served on a platter before him, waiting to be consumed. She was exposed, and it scared the hell out of her, however, at the same time, it thrilled her. She was addicted to the sensation that came with being around Will. Every touch, lick, bite...it consumed her.

She needed clarity to understand what it was, exactly, the men asked of her. They wanted her, that much was clear, and she wanted them. All of them...at the same time. Never in her life had she considered such a thing possible.

Lying in her bed, the sheets warm

under her body, she glanced over at the curtains and wondered what time of the day it was. Was it morning? Night? She had no recollection of time.

Leaving the confines of her bed, the floor chilled her feet and a chill surrounded her body. She grasped the comforter from the bed and wrapped it around her naked body. Subtle flurries warmed her belly when she thought of her men ravaging her body as the soreness settled into her legs, between her thighs, backside, and her neck.

A heat crept up her neck and she smiled. No one had ever given her as much pleasure as she experienced with them. No one else ever would. They accomplished their goal in ruining her for anyone else. The thought made her chuckle.

She reached for the curtain and drew it back. The sun had begun to crest over the horizon, mixing soft hues of blue with the darkness of the night. Soon the bright orb would be full in the sky. She longed to feel the heated rays on her skin. If this was the life she chose, it would not be often she could sunbathe, garden, run a marathon. Not that she would run a marathon, but if she wanted to. She didn't think any were held at night.

Closing her eyes, she inhaled the smells of the morning; fresh dew on the ground, grass, the fall foliage. She sighed and leaned against the rails on her balcony.

She looked down at her arms, at the remaining red marks where two of her men had bitten into her flesh. She touched the strawberry spots, the skin tender under her fingers. The flesh tingled, and a flutter of excitement shot through her body.

Tawne had four vampires. *Four.* They were hers and she... She wasn't sure what she was in this moment. She was human, not a demon, not a vampire. Human.

But not for long. The words echoed through her mind once more.

What did the men expect of her? Did they expect her to take this serum Chayton had created? Would it change her chemical makeup and make her a demon? Would it kill her and she'd be reborn as a demon? What of her human life? Would she be removed from all human society? What about children? Vampires could not create children, unlike some of the tales woven throughout fiction history. She wasn't sure about children, but had not completely written off having them, either. But accepting this life and everything that came with it meant giving all of this up...and children.

She gripped the rail and stared up at the morning sky. Her heart sped to a quickened beat and her chest grew tight. She coughed, having a tough time breathing. Gasping for air, she let go of the comforter and it dropped to the ground around her. Tawne was out in the open but she had never felt so enclosed...trapped.

"I need to go. I need air, to get out of here. I need..." she paused in her mumbling and backed away from the rail. "Home."

Panic. She recognized the symptoms and closed her eyes, sucking in long, deep breaths. She shivered and after opening her eyes, she looked down at herself. She stood naked on the balcony, panicking about drinking a serum and giving up her life. She was being ridiculous, or maybe it was delirium. Time would definitely tell.

***

Tawne put on the clothes she'd worn

to the vampire's home and made her way to the balcony window. It was later in the afternoon. Soon the men would bring up the topic of the serum and ask if she'd take it. Could she take it? Of course, she could make rational decisions, but would she? Not likely. How to tell the men who had changed her life and turned it upside down? She was clueless on how to broach that subject.

Hey, yeah, I like you and all, and wow, you fucked me really good, but no, I can't do this.

Or maybe...

I'm a human and I can't live in your society just like you can't live in mine. I'm out.

Or maybe...

You're the best thing that's ever happened to me in my lonely world and I can't wait to join you.

Door number three sounded best and she wanted it, but did she need it? She had no idea. The men were bouncing around in her head. Cristofano, Evan, Chayton, and Will. Their forms were corporeal, but only slightly. Their forms moved with the wind that blew through the imagination of her mind.

She sighed and grabbed her purse. She needed to get out before her emotions forced her to change her mind.

She'd just closed her bedroom door behind her when a loud clap of thunder erupted, and she jumped, fear coursing through her. A flash of lightning lit the sky briefly and the familiar tap-tap-tap on the roof alerted her it was raining.

Fucking perfect.

Not wanting to make a sound walking the stairs, she decided to take the elevator. She peeked around the hall area and found it empty. She took a deep breath, then made her way to the lift. She pressed the button and felt relief the instant the doors opened. Tawne stepped inside and pressed the first floor button. As the doors closed, thunder clapped again, but his time it was louder, closer.

The elevator began to move, descending down. Was leaving the right decision? If she wanted to remain human and hold onto the possibility of having children, then yes. She glanced up at the ceiling and through her mind's eye, willed herself to see her four men, staring back at her.

Tawne closed her eyes and a tear slipped down her cheek. The moment something good came into her life, it was only a matter of time before it was ripped away.

First her parents, then Olivia left her for a while. She came back, but it wasn't the same. She wasn't the same. Anyone who'd ever loved Tawne left her. Yet, here were four men, asking for her to stay, and all she could do was leave.

Another thunderclap disrupted her

self-mutilating thoughts. The elevator jolted, and the light went out. She screamed and fell to her knees, dropping her purse. Her chest ached as her heartbeat surged in rhythm with panic and adrenaline.

Short breaths pushed past her lips and her hands shook underneath her. She couldn't hold her body up much longer and her arms collapsed. She fell to her side and pulled her knees to her chest.

Tawne closed her eyes and rocked on the floor. She sobbed and cried out, "Help me!"

"Tawne?"

She heard a voice call for her, but wasn't sure if it was one of her men, or her mind playing tricks.

"Tawne, are you in the elevator?" It was Evan. "Tawne, please answer me!"

She squeaked, but nothing more. She couldn't talk, breathe, or move. The sound of her cell phone chimed in the darkness. The phone was in her purse, but she couldn't move. If she moved, the elevator might fall, and she would die. That's all there was to it.

"Tawne, we need to know you're okay. Please, answer!"

We? Who all was outside? It didn't matter, she wouldn't move. She cried, tears flowed from her in waves. Pain squeezed her chest and she hissed.

"I can feel you, Tawne." It was Will. "Your pain shot through each of us. You're going to be fine. I promise."

"Just breathe, Tawne." This time it was Chayton. Were they all waiting for her?

The elevator jolted again, and panic screamed through her, sending a shrill from her that would give a banshee a run for their money.

"She's near the second floor," Cristofano announced. "Let's get the doors opened and get her the fuck out."

"Fuck this," she heard Will growl. Then he groaned as if he were squeezing something hard, or maybe pulling.

Light leaked in, disrupting the blackness of the confined space. It grew wider and she lifted her gaze up to it. It was like Heaven, here to claim their angel.

But she was no angel, not like this. It wasn't like her men were angels either. The thought made her want to laugh in the middle of her breakdown.

The door opened more, and she could see Will on the other side, straining to get it open. More hands pushed and finally, the door gave and opened fully.

Like an animal in danger, she rushed out the elevator on her hands and knees, and into the strong arms of a man. She sobbed into a strong, comforting chest, having no idea who she clung to, but she didn't care. She cried into his chest and fisted his shirt in her hands.

He cradled her head and he pressed his lips to her forehead. "Shh, I have you. You'll be all right. You're safe."

She lifted her gaze, blurred and tear ridden, to stare into the eyes of Will.

He smiled and wiped the tears from her face. "We have you."

She closed her eyes and rested her forehead against his chest. "I'm sorry," she whispered.

"What are you sorry about?" Cristofano asked and laid his hands on her shoulders.

Her heart broke and the words were on the tip of her tongue. As much as she wanted to tell them why, she wanted to take the words back. She pulled herself free from Will and waved off the men from trying to touch or coddle her. She met their gazes and lied.

"I didn't mean to scare you. One of my worst fears is falling to my death in an elevator."

Chayton took a step forward and reached for her hands. "You're safe now. There's something we wanted to show you when you're ready."

"Yes," Evan added. "Let's take a minute and relax with a drink, get ourselves cleaned up, and head out."

"Where are we going?" She glanced at Evan, then Chayton. She was about to tell them she couldn't do this but decided against it. Were they none the wiser? Did they know? Could they feel it? Pushing her feelings aside, she forced a smile. "What's the plan?"

Cristofano stepped closer and took one of her hands from Chayton. "Consider it a surprise, setup with the coven."

She raised her brows. "A surprise with the coven? Wow...that's kind of huge, right?"

Cristofano nodded. "Yes, definitely. With the promise of this new serum, we think the sky is the limit." His smile resonated in his eyes. She couldn't help but smile back.

And a part of her died inside. She was a shit. No, not a shit—the shit that grew on dog shit when it was hot outside. She was the scum that fed the nasty crust that grew around dog shit.

This was not the ending of her fairytale story she'd planned for herself. Her eyes burned with a new threat of tears. She fought like hell to keep them hidden.

"Wow, I can't wait."

Chapter Fifteen

THEY SAY THE love of money is the root
of all evil and it doesn't buy happiness.
Whoever said that didn't have a
bottomless pit for a wallet. They also
didn't have everything you never knew
you wanted until it was placed on display
before you.

Tawne stepped out of the limo in front
of a warehouse district. Realizing it was
the same place where Olivia had them
meet not so long ago, she frowned. She
turned to Cristofano as he exited the car

behind her. The others had remained behind for this part of the trip. The sun had already set, but it didn't stop the vampire from wearing sunglasses.

She grinned. "You know you don't need those, right?"

He chuckled. His white teeth and fangs shimmered in the iridescent light of the full moon. His gray business suit was almost black in the darkness. He lowered the shades to the middle of his nose and looked at her over the rims. "Don't take away my fun, my love."

The man was crack for a sex addict. Sexy-as-sin in the darkest way possible, yet, each had a light about them that promised safety, security, and promise.

Cristofano winked and pushed his glasses back onto his face. "Come on, we'll be late if you continue to stare at me with those hungry eyes."

"I have no idea what you're talking about," she whispered with a giggle. She turned to face the warehouses and the night her world changed came rushing back to her. Everything she knew, and believed, had shattered that evening.

"What's the matter?" he asked her.

She shook her head. The same feeling she had in the elevator came rushing back. Her chest clinched, and her heartbeat sped in rhythm. "I—I don't know." She damn well knew what it was, but she couldn't admit to one of the men who had shown nothing but adoration for her. She stepped into their lives and they wanted nothing more than to give her everything, be everything she could ever need, even if it meant no longer being human.

She swallowed the dryness in her throat as he took her hand.

"Come, it won't be so bad, I promise. Inside looks much different than out. Every quarter the coven hosts a pairing ceremony. The next one is in a few days.

If it were not for you, my love, we would be part of the ceremony."

That was almost hard to hear. They expected she would take this serum Chayton was working on and she would become their concubine, just like Olivia had for her men. But was this what she really wanted? Did she want this life?

She looked back at the car they'd arrived in as the driver pulled away toward a parking area, lights still on.

Well, at least he didn't leave.

When she remained silent, Cristofano continued. "There's a surprise inside waiting for you," Cristofano announced. "I think you'll be quite pleased."

"Is that so?" Tawne glanced up at the man, then stopped in her steps. "Wait," she whispered. "I need a minute."

"What's the matter, my love?" He touched her chin with a finger and lifted her head up.

She avoided looking into his eyes,

keeping them trained on the beard covering his cheeks and chin.

"Talk to me, what is it?"

She took his hand and pulled it away from her face, then forced a smile. She met his gaze and took a step back. "Nothing. Let's go inside. I'm curious about this pairing Olivia has talked so much about."

He nodded, pulled her hand into the crook of his elbow and proceeded forward. The light from the parking lot lampposts faded into the shadows of the building. Soon, they stood before a painted red door. He knocked three times on the solid wood and they waited.

The door unlocked, and it creaked open. Fear shot through her and she squeezed Cristofano's arm.

"My love," he whispered, "you're perfectly safe. No harm will come to you here, or anywhere while you're with us."

She nodded and tucked herself in

closer to his body. The inside of the building did not settle her fear any. There was only darkness on the other side of the door. That was, until a light flicked on.

A woman on the other side peeked through. She was beautiful with pixie styled blonde hair, light blue eyes, and pale skin. She smiled, and fangs tipped on the edge of her soft pink lips.

"Hello, Cristofano. I'm happy you made it with your friend." The woman looked at Tawne and opened the door further. "This is indeed a treat! We have never catered to humans. You are most welcome, Mistress Tawne."

Tawne grinned. "Thank you, I appreciate that." She wasn't sure what else to say. In a way, she felt like a sheep being presented at a conference for vegan lions, but only recently converted to this new way of eating. She took a deep breath and followed along with

Cristofano.

The heavy door closed behind them and the woman led the way toward another door. "My name is Sasha." She turned to look at Tawne and smiled. "Anything you may need tonight, I'm happy to help."

"Thank you, Sasha," Tawne answered. If she wanted to quickly exit, she wasn't sure Sasha was the best person to ask. She at least knew of this door to leave, but there had to be others inside as well.

The next door opened and Tawne held her breath. She wasn't sure what to expect on the other side, but when the door opened fully, it was not anything like she expected. She thought she would walk into a chamber of wooden crosses the size of humans. She would be tied to it and drained, then her blood replaced with this synthetic substance Chayton made. It was barbaric, but it was what her mind was putting on display for her.

Rather than something like a dungeon, the room opened into a grand ballroom. Red velvet walls with lined art from familiar artists, tables with chairs and centerpieces, and in the middle it was empty. Maybe a dance floor?

Above the open space hung a chandelier of crystal. She could not imagine how much that would have cost but admired the lights as they danced off the walls and the floor. Everything inside this room, this warehouse, was stunning.

She smiled and let go of Cristofano's arm.

"Not quite what you expected?"

She turned to an unfamiliar voice. A man glided with the air as if he floated and stood next to Cristofano. He was someone she had not met before now. The man had raven colored, shoulder length hair, parted down the middle. It looked as soft as silk and hung bone straight. She could imagine what it would feel like as it trailed over her fingers. He smiled at her, and like the others, his fangs were displayed.

"Love, this is Malik. He's one of the leaders in our coven. Malik, this is Tawne O'Brien, the human we spoke of on the phone."

Tawne glanced between the men, then took note of Sasha as she stood toward the back of the room. Was she something like wait staff? Maybe a bodyguard? She looked back at Malik and offered a shy smile.

"It's nice to meet you. I've heard much about you and the coven."

He chuckled and held his hand out for her, and she took it. "Well, pray tell, I hope it was all good."

His hand was soft, and somewhat cold, but he was pleasant. "Yes, all good."

"Perfect. Now, Miss Tawne, if I may be so bold, I understand you were studying history? Maybe looking to become a museum curator?"

She raised her brows. "How did you..." she trailed off and caught Cristofano smirking. She lifted one corner of her mouth into a grin. "Yes, sir. My ambition is to restore artifacts and become a curator of a museum. I love history and all that comes with it." She removed her hand from his.

"That is wonderful to hear. It also just happens that we have a position open here with our coven for such a role."

Tawne took a step back. "What?"

"That's right," Cristofano answered. "All of this can be yours, if you want it."

Her mouth agape, she was lost for words. She would have to have worked for years to build up credibility and establish herself as a professional just to get in the door at a museum. Yet, here they were, offering her what she wanted on a silver platter...with a syringe filled with a substance to change her chemical makeup.

Everything comes with a price.

She again forced a smile. "I...I don't know what to say."

"Say yes," Cristofano whispered to her. "All of this, and all of us, will be yours."

"All I have to do is sign my life away and become something I'm not."

Silence passed between the three and Malik cleared his throat. "I will leave you two to talk this over." He turned to leave and after a few steps, he paused. "I heard from Chayton just before your arrival. He has finished the serum."

Tawne closed her eyes and turned away from the men and faced an open space of tables, red walls, and light dancing around the room.

Everything she could have ever wanted was laid out before her. Money, wanting for nothing, a life of luxury, her love of history and restoration of artifacts. All she had to do was become an artificial blood demon.

A tear slid down her cheek and she quickly swiped it away. A pair of hands rested on her shoulders and Cristofano stood just behind her, his chest touching her back. "My love, I am picking up melancholy from you. What's the matter?"

"I..." she couldn't get herself to finish. Instead, she shook her head.

"Is this not everything you wanted?"

"It is," she whispered.

"Then what's wrong?"

She turned to face him and took a step back. "Everything is wrong. This. All of this is wrong. You can't buy me, Cris. I feel like I'm being bought like that actress in that hooker movie where a rich man swept her off her feet. Life doesn't work like that."

"*Pretty woman?*"

"What?"

"The movie. *Pretty woman.*"

She sighed and nodded. "Yes. *Pretty Woman*." She looked into his eyes. A part of her died just then. He looked like a hurt puppy and it killed her. "I just need time. All of this has been rushed and thrust upon me. I don't know if I'm ready for all of this."

"No one is rushing you into a decision, my love."

Her mouth opened in shock. "Is that not what all this is for?"

"Yes, and no. This is to offer you something to do if you chose to stay with us. We would not dare keep you captive inside our home for all eternity. With your love of history and restorations, the coven actually required a team to do this work for them. When the knowledge was passed over to Malik on what you desired, he made sure you would be well compensated. And not just a monetary value. He wanted to make sure you had everything you would ever need with this new role.

"You being here with us is also new to the coven. You being here is changing the face of everything we have ever known and believed. Chayton is making history with this serum. You could be the first human to serve as a concubine to vampires. I need you to understand the importance of this."

She nodded. "I do. I understand, but I also need you to understand the hardship this is putting on me. I'll be giving up my life as human to be your concubine. I'll never have children or grandchildren. I don't know if that is something I can live with."

Cristofano lowered his gaze to the ground and nodded. "I see." He turned his back to her and headed toward the door. He paused with a sigh, then glanced over his shoulder to her. "Come. We'll drive back home, and I'll discuss what we talked about tonight with my brothers. If you choose to leave, it will be your decision and yours alone. No one will come to you to try and convince you to stay. Honestly, we shouldn't have to try to convince you." He grabbed the door and turned back once more. "It is not often one finds the love of their life by a chance encounter. Add to that three additional bodies who feel the same way I do. Love is love, Tawne. It's only up to you to accept what may be the best thing that has ever come into your life. Monster or not."

Cristofano opened the door and passed through it. When it closed behind him, Tawne pulled out one of the chairs at the table and sat down. She held her head in her hand and let everything she had been feeling, go.

Pain. Misery. Happiness. Lust. Angst. Power.

Yes, she felt powerful with her men. No one had ever made her feel this way in the past. She would always change herself for the person she dated until their true colors showed. But then again, didn't she do the same thing?

These men, these vampires, hid nothing. Will, desperate and powerful Will. He surprised her most of all. He didn't put up a false bravado. He was an asshole and had every right to feel the way he did...until he took a chance on Tawne.

And here she was, an even bigger asshole, walking out of their lives.

"I can't do this." She stood and looked over to where Sasha stood. "I need a ride, please."

Chapter Sixteen

WHEN THE WORLD collapses and all you can do to survive is watch everything fall to its demise, in slow motion, while you hold onto the hope someone will find you before all the rubble buries you completely.

Tawne stared out the bedroom window of her condo. Winter had arrived in New Orleans. A cold front blew through and with it, icy roads and car accidents. Sirens screamed in the distance while another hurt person was taken by ambulance. She tugged her robe closer around her body and rocked in her rocking chair.

None of it phased her. She had been home for what...one, two weeks? She wasn't even sure anymore. She knew the rules: stay in their world and learn everything you can, but if you leave, your mind will be wiped of the memories.

She tugged the sleeve of her robe up and glanced down at the barely there strawberry marks on her skin. Cristofano fed there. On her opposite arm, it was Chayton. She thought of Evan and the scar on the inside of her thigh. Then there was Will. He left his mark on the side of her neck.

With a sigh, she pulled the sleeve back down her arm once more. She was ready to have her memory wiped. She didn't want to deal with the emotions, the disappointment she caused not only her men but also her best friend, Olivia. But how could they expect her to go through with this? She had just met them, and they wanted her to change her life for them.

Who does that?

People in love, that's who. You become anything, everything for them.

She closed her eyes and rested her head back on the chair. A tear slipped down her cheek and an ache had formed in her chest. She rubbed just above her heart and her bottom lip trembled. Then her body shook and Tawne began to sob.

She cried for the love she continued to deny herself. For the feelings that had developed in such a short period of time. For the excitement the men brought her, and for the opportunity of a lifetime to work alongside vampires restoring artifacts...and to become part of their history.

She had thrown it all away because—

A knock at the door sounded and she

sat up. Wiping her face with her sleeves, she stood and crossed the room. Peeking through the door hole, she didn't recognize the person on the other side. Having a hood over their head and sunglasses on...at night...didn't help, either.

"Who is it?"

The person removed the glasses and lowered the hoodie. It was a female. She looked up to the peephole and Tawne gasped. It was Sasha, the vampire she'd met at the coven's warehouse the other week.

"What can I do for you, Sasha?" Tawne hadn't opened the door yet but leaned against it instead. She wanted to open the door and pull the woman into a hug, just to get a sense of what she'd left behind. She decided against it since she didn't really know Sasha. The woman might fight her off or worse, bite her.

She thought of her men and her heart

ached even harder.

"You know why I'm here. Please, open the door unless you want me to announce in the hallway why I'm really here."

Tawne sighed and unlocked her door. She opened it enough to look at Sasha. She tried to smile, but it faded as quickly as it formed. "Hi."

"Hi," Sasha repeated. "May I come in?"

Tawne nodded and opened the door wider. "Please, come inside." Once Sasha passed through, she closed the door behind her and locked it. "Are they with you?"

Sasha turned to face her and shook her head. "No, just me and my driver."

"Okay," Tawne answered. "You're here about my memory bank, huh?"

Sasha nodded. "Yup. If you want to talk some before we do this, we can. Sometimes people want to be heard, kind of like a last supper type thing."

Tawne raised her brows. "That's a very bad comparison. Last supper was before Jesus' death."

Sasha grinned. "No one's killing you Tawne." She chuckled. "I'm only saying some like to discuss what could have been before leaving it all behind. Would you like to do that?"

Tawne shook her head and headed toward the couch. "Come, have a seat. Do you want some tea or water or anything?"

Sasha grinned and shook her head. "No, thank you."

"Oh, right. Blood," Tawne whispered. "Well, how does this work?"

Sasha didn't answer at first; she only stared into Tawne's eyes. "The men need you back with them."

Tawne took note of the word *need*, not want. She lowered her gaze to the carpeted floor. "I don't think I can do it, Sasha. They're asking me to give up everything I am and become something I'm not."

She touched Tawne's cheek. "Have you considered adding to who you are and changing nothing? No one would ever expect you to be something you're not."

"But I'm not a blood demon. And what do you mean, add to who I am?"

Sasha released her and crossed one leg over the other, then placed her hands in her lap. "Let's pull on a religious experience again. When I was a human, my father was a preacher."

"Oh, that explains the last supper reference."

Sasha smiled. "Sure, but what I'm saying is this: when a person decides to be good, they don't necessarily change who they are. They add to it. For instance, if you wanted to start going to church because you knew you needed a different direction in your life, you'd start out small and find a church that suited your needs. Right?"

Tawne listened to what she was talking about and nodded. "I'll be honest with you. It's been ages since I've been to church."

"That's not the point. Just a reference to understand where I'm coming from. Okay, so let's say you started going to church. You met some new people. They delivered sermons you could identify with. You're not sure how you identify, but there's something in it that just touches you. You feel it and you realize, you need more of that.

"You begin to feel something bigger than yourself. Something greater is working through you. You open yourself to the possibility of it because it feels right. Suddenly, things in life are no longer so bad. With that reflection, the bad things you used to do begin to fade away and in its place, the good you've learned to love."

Tawne fidgeted in her seat and gave a soft shrug. "I understand what you're trying to say here, I really do, but what does this have to do with me and my vampires?"

Sasha smiled. "I won't pretend you didn't say *my vampires*."

"I did?"

Sasha nodded. "Okay, so let's say the church was the coven and the people you've met are your vampires. You feel comfort with them. You know there's something great at work here, and you really want to explore the options. As an added bonus, you have the career of your dreams right at your fingertips. Everything you could have ever wanted is right in front of you."

She began to count on her fingers. "Love from four men who would completely devote themselves to you, be anything you need. You'd never want for anything. There's a position with the coven to do what you love. And lastly, the opportunity to make history with us."

"It all sounds so glamorous, but I'm afraid that's exactly what it is; just glamour. When reality finally hits, will I think I've made a mistake?"

"How do we know when we walk down the aisle we've made a mistake marrying the person we've vowed to spend the rest of our lives with?"

Tawne raised her brows. "Good point."

"I'm trying to tell you that there are options in this life. You decide what you want, they don't decide for you."

"What about children? They cannot create babies. What if I wanted to have children?"

Sasha leaned in and grasped her hand. "What in the world made you believe the right to have children was taken away from you?"

Tawne's mouth opened agape. "Are you saying they can get me pregnant?"

The other woman chuckled. "Heavens, no. What I'm saying is, there's ways of getting you pregnant. A Sperm bank is one option."

She felt like a damned fool. With a sigh, she pulled her hand free and looked at her lap. "I wish I would have known all this before."

"Tawne," Sasha started. "Did you ask anyone?"

She shook her head. "Hell, no. I just assumed."

"Do you still want to be on your own and forget all of what you've experienced, or would you like to go back and accept this new life?"

Tawne met her gaze and a new hope rose inside her. "You mean, I can still go back?"

Sasha nodded. "You're not the first woman to decline an offer as a concubine. Well, first human, but not the first woman."

"So, what you're saying is nothing has to necessarily change. I can still be me and hold onto my dreams of restoring artifacts and becoming a curator."

Sasha nodded. "That is exactly what I'm telling you. All that will be different, other than your lifestyle, is you'll move in with your men."

"Damn, I'm such a fucktard bitch."

Sasha laughed. "Well, that's a first. Not sure I've ever heard those words put together before."

"Oh, believe me, I have more," Tawne told her. "When does the pairing start for the men? In another week or something?"

Sasha frowned and shook her head. "No, Tawne. It's starting right now. The men are expected to choose a blood demon tonight."

"Fuck," she whispered and stood. She paced and ran her hand through her hair, feeling frantic. "What the fuck did I do? What do I do now, Sasha? What do I do?"

Sasha stood and clutched Tawne's hand, stopping her from pacing. "You get yourself cleaned up and I'll drive you to the ceremony. That is what you'll do. Well, that is, if this is really what you want?"

"Fuck, yes!" Tawne screamed and ran toward her bedroom. "Give me twenty minutes!"

"Better make it ten," Sasha hollered back.

Tawne squealed when she ran into her bedroom. Why she didn't think of the points Sasha brought up before was beyond her. She felt dense and stupid.

Put a hat on me and put me in the dunce corner.

She grabbed a cocktail dress from her closet, one that she loved and had worn only one time. She did a quick job on cleaning up and applied her makeup. She pulled on her dress and brushed her blonde hair into a ponytail, then twisted it around into a bun. She grabbed heels with faux diamond encrusted butterflies on the front and pulled them on. Making her way to the living room, she applied a layer of lipstick then smacked her lips together.

"How do I look?"

"You clean up nice. Now, let's get you there before any chance on reclaiming your men is lost."

"Shit, can we call them?"

Sasha shook her head. "This is a very old ceremony. It would be rude to take calls during a paring."

"Crap." She pulled her phone out and dialed Olivia's number. It immediately went to voicemail. Would Olivia even be there?

"I can feel your panic. Your friend will be there with her men. Once we get you inside, you can find her and explain what happened if you want."

Tawne nodded. "I'd rather get a message to her first, though, but it seems her phone isn't on." She pulled the messages off her phone and sent a text to Olivia.

Please don't let my guys choose. I'm on my way. I fucked up royally and I'm with Sasha. She's bringing me back. Please, Liv, please. Don't let them choose.

She hit send and shoved her phone into her purse. "Let's go save the life I just threw away."

Chapter Seventeen

TAWNE AND SASHA made it back to the mansion just as the sky turned a dark wine color. The stars were bright, and the full moon glowed with a soft outline surrounding it. The night was chilly as winter had arrived. The breeze blew from the gulf carrying with it the smell of salt in the air, as well as the wildlife in the sea.

"Come on, we have maybe an hour before it's too late," Sasha announced as she parked in the driveway of her men's home.

They exited the car and Sasha pressed a few buttons on a keypad, and the door unlocked.

"You know the keypad code?"

"In case of emergencies, I have access to everyone's information."

"Ahh, well this is good to know. And also makes you a little dangerous."

Sasha grinned and waved Tawne inside. "Let's move. *Vamonos!*"

Tawne glanced her way and furrowed her brows. "You know Spanish?"

"I know many languages. What does this have to do with getting you to the pairing?"

"Right," Tawne whispered and looked down the corridor to the elevator. "Not today, Satan." She made her way toward the stairs instead.

"Do I even want to know what that was about?" Sasha asked.

Tawne shook her head. "I'm positive

you'll hear about it later."

The human and the vampire sped down the stairs to the basement floor and walked into Chayton's lab. Tawne wondered for a moment if Sasha was taking her time to not bolt down the stairs with her vampire speed. She felt even more respect for the woman and knew, in time, she may grow to become a best friend. Not quite like a sister, like Olivia was, but someone very close she could consider a confident.

"Here we are," Tawne announced and did her best to not sound winded. She wanted to kick her own ass for not getting on her treadmill more often, but who has time for that with four hot-as-hell vampires on your tail at all times?

Fuck exercise.

Tawne turned on the lights to the lab. "Do you know what the substance looks like?"

Sasha nodded. "Yes, and I know

Chayton put the successful batch in the cooler." She walked across the room to the stainless steel fridge.

Sasha opened the door and the light spilled out onto the floor casting a shadow around her body. "Here we go."

She closed the door and turned around. In her hand, she held a slender tube. It reminded Tawne of the shots from the bars she went to in her early twenties.

Sasha handed the vial forward, then hesitated and pulled it back. "Are you ready for this?"

Tawne nodded. "Yes, yes, I am. I want this."

"You want it or *need* it? There is a very defined difference."

Tawne sighed and rested her hands on her hips. "Stop fucking with my head. I want the fucking serum, so I can be with my men. I... Hell, I love them, Sasha. I have no idea why I do, but I do. My life was not complete until they were in it. I had a void in my heart and I knew when I met them, they would fill the hole. And they did."

"That's what she said." Sasha giggled.

"You're incorrigible," Tawne said with a shake of her head, then she smirked. "Okay, Sasha, give me the vial."

The vampire handed over the slender tube.

It was cold between Tawne's fingers. She pulled the cork lid off the top, then looked at Sasha. "So, I just drink?"

"Yes, bottoms up."

Tawne turned the tube upside down and drained the contents into her mouth. It tasted like the fizzy stomach drink taken after a night out with Jim and Johnny Walker. She swallowed and swiped her mouth with the back of her hand.

"Do you feel anything?"

Tawne shook her head. "Other than

the stuff being nasty as fuck?"

Sasha laughed. "You'll be happy to know Chayton has been working on this for a long, long time."

"How did he test it?"

Sasha lifted a brow. "How do you think?"

Tawne made an 'O' with her lips then set the tube on the table next to her. "Should I feel anything?"

With a shrug, Sasha stepped forward. "We need to get going if we're going to do this."

Tawne nodded. "Yes, I know. I just thought—"

She bent over and groaned. Her stomach erupted in a pain worse than a stomach virus.

"Tawne?" Alarmed, Sasha was by her side in a second. "What's happening?"

"I don't know," she managed to groan. "Fuck... I'm dying, holy shit make it stop!"

"No, you have to let it run its course. Your blood, your essence, everything about you is changing, Tawne. Everything. Give it a moment, it will soon pass."

"How do you know? Holy mother of all things Hell!" She started to drop to her knees when Sasha caught her.

"It's what happened on the other test subjects."

"Outstanding," she growled. "How many did he test on?"

"Does it matter?" Sasha answered.

"Yes. I want to know what happened to them after the transition."

"They survived. Isn't that all that matters?"

Tawne glared at the woman. "There's a difference between surviving and living."

Sasha smiled and straightened Tawne to a standing position. "Two minutes, max, and you'll be just fine. As for surviving, yes. They did just fine. We had volunteers come in to test the serum. Once it took, vampires with no concubine tasted their blood until the serum was complete. Your blood will be synthetic. Like a meat eater choosing tofu for the rest of their life by choice."

"Lovely. I've just been compared to steak!"

"You must be feeling better to crack a joke. Tell me, is it passing?"

Tawne nodded, then met Sasha's gaze. She frowned. "Something's different. You look...no, you smell different."

Sasha smiled. "Then it's definitely working. You're not a blood demon, but your body believes it now is. You'll be drawn even more to your vampires now, and them to you. They'll be able to feed on you without help from a volunteer." She leaned in. "Have Olivia tell you her story one day when she almost attacked a volunteer named Candace once."

Tawne arched a brow. "I'll keep that in

mind." She sucked in a long breath, then slowly exhaled. "Everything smells different. No, not different, just stronger."

"That's normal. You'll probably see and hear better as well. Oh!" Sasha released the grip she had on Tawne and continued. "Just wait until you have sex and they bite you!"

She smiled, and her cheeks burned with embarrassment. "I can't wait. Can we go now?"

Sasha nodded. "Yes! Let's go. We have," she checked her phone, "shit! We have minutes! Let's go!"

***

Tawne buzzed with anticipation. She was a nervous ball of excitement and a part of her was also scared to death of rejection. What if she showed up and the men turned their backs on her? Or worse, the coven wouldn't allow her entrance after she'd left?

She hadn't given any words, or reasons, for her departure, just bolted. Everyone in her life always left her; whether that was by death or on their own accord, no one ever stayed long enough to give a damn. Now, there were four men willing to lay down their lives for her, and to show her appreciation, she shit on them, then left.

There was no way she would be welcomed back. She bent over in her seat and held her face in her hands.

"What's the matter?" Sasha asked and placed her hand on Tawne's back.

"I'm kidding myself that the coven and my men will have anything to do with me. I left without a word. I got scared and fled."

"Don't you think they realized that?"

She shook her head and looked at the woman next to her. Beautiful and confident, Sasha was everything Tawne wasn't. Tall, slender, blonde, and beautiful, where Tawne was short, with blonde hair and on the heavier side.

"Don't do that," Sasha scolded.

"What did I do?"

"Don't act like you don't know. The mood just did a serious shift from sadness to angst. Don't compare yourself to me. You have no idea what I've been through to get to this point in my life."

Tawne lowered her gaze. "I'm sorry, I didn't mean any offense."

"None taken." Sasha touched just under Tawne's chin and lifted her face up. "Don't you think your men love you for you?"

She shrugged. "Well, I hope it's not because I'm a meal ticket."

Sasha growled and the sound actually frightened Tawne. She scooted away from her in her seat. "Why don't you try that again."

"I'm sorry!" Tawne pleaded. "My self-defense has always been humor. I didn't mean any offense, I promise."

Sasha lifted her brow. "The men went through a lot to get to where they are. They opted to be the first to try a human female rather than a blood demon."

"May I ask why?" She just realized she had not asked this before and wanted to kick herself for it.

Sasha nodded. "Our incubus are a dying breed. We still have about a thousand active, but it's not enough. Not every one of them produce offspring. To tell you the truth, some of our vampires have been starving. Chayton creating this serum will save many lives and open the doors for many more to come. Not just humans."

She lifted a brow. "Are you telling me there's shifters and other demons in the world?"

Sasha smiled, then laughed. "You think vampires and blood demons are the only creatures in the world to walk alongside humans?"

"Well, with the question for my question, I'll say no."

"Good answer. And, we're here."

The car pulled to a stop in the familiar warehouse district. Opening the doors, Tawne exited and double checked herself.

Dress.

Shoes.

Hair.

Makeup.

Bra and panties.

She looked to Sasha. "Will you walk me in?"

The vampire nodded. "Of course, but the entrance must only be you, and you must be announced."

Tawne felt her stomach drop. "Fuck me. I have no one to do this for me."

She smiled. "Yes, you do." She pulled her phone out and pressed a few buttons, then brought the phone to her ear. "Hey, yeah it's me. Listen, I have a huge favor. Meet me out back. Yes, she's here. She's ready. Will you escort her inside? I owe you one. Bye." She hung up with a smile.

"Well?"

"You have an escort. I wish you the best. I'll walk you to him, but from that point he'll be your guide."

"Hi, ladies."

Tawne turned to the familiar voice and found Jesse approaching. She smiled. "Hi. Thank you so much for doing this."

"I'm glad to see you back. You ready?" He held his arm out for her.

She took it and nodded. "Yes, I am ready. I sure as hell hope they're ready for me."

He chuckled. "I'm sure they'll be surprised, but in a good way."

Sasha walked ahead of the two and paused in front of the double doors. "I'm going to open these, then there will be another set of doors. When you pass through them, you'll recognize the room. Do not speak until you're spoken to. Understand?"

Tawne nodded.

"Usually that's my line," Jesse told her.

She stuck her tongue out at him, then opened the doors.

Tawne sucked in a deep breath when they stepped inside, then exhaled when the doors closed behind them, plunging them into darkness. The second set of doors opened, and light cut into the shadows.

The chattering and drinking came to a dull buzz and most everyone in the room turned to see who the late newcomer was.

"May I present," Sasha roared with her voice. "Miss Tawne O'Brien."

"Tawne?"

She heard Olivia somewhere in the room, then the strike of heels as they ran across the floor. Through the crowd, Olivia pushed her way through and, eyes wide with surprise, smiled.

Chapter Eighteen

THEY SAY THE scariest dreams are those where you're in front of a classroom naked, but you don't realize you're naked until you look down.

Tawne had had a fright and wanted to make sure she was not dreaming. She glanced down and saw she was dressed and knew, without a doubt, she was not dreaming. This was, indeed, happening.

She stood frozen and gripped Jesse's arm. "What do I do?" she asked through gritted teeth.

"Follow my lead," he whispered.

Following in step with Jesse, they approached Olivia. The two women stared at one another, unmoving.

"I'm so glad you're here," Olivia whispered.

Tawne nodded with a smile and batted her lashes. She would cry if she didn't control her feelings.

"They're here, all of them, but they have not been presented to the concubines as of yet. Consider yourself on time."

Tawne smiled and bowed her head once to show her appreciation.

"You look amazing, by the way," Jesse whispered. "They will be in for a surprise when they see you."

She smiled and kept her eyes straight ahead. The red velvet walls had scones aflame, providing a soft hue of golden light. The chandelier shimmered radiance across the room. A violin played in the distance.

A set of doors opened across the room.

"And, so it begins," Jesse told her.

She held tight onto his arm and realized she stood in a large circle with the other women being presented to the vampires. Two at a time, men walked into the center of the room and spread out, taking in all the women.

She felt like a woman up for auction. It was almost uncomfortable having never experienced this before, but this had been their way of life for centuries. For them, it was normal. For her, it was up there with brand-new-never-to-do-again.

Then she saw Cristofano, Evan, Chayton, and last, her Will. She smiled wide and her heartbeat rushed in its rhythm. She wanted to scream out for them to see her but fought against it.

Her men talked amongst themselves. One would nod, the other shake his head. What were they discussing? Who to pick up? Were they talking about her?

Look at me, I'm here. I'm here!

She had been so focused on her men, Tawne didn't realize she had been approached.

"What's your name?"

"What?" She looked at the man and shook her head.

"The lady declined. Thank you," Jesse informed him.

The man shrugged. She followed him with her gaze, then looked back at Cristofano, and froze. He'd found her and was staring at her as if she were a lifeline to his dying body. In a way, she was just that.

She smiled and placed her hand over her lips. She didn't want to scream or cry out. Instead, her knees weakened, and Jesse wrapped an arm around her body.

"Hold yourself up, Tawne. This isn't over yet."

She nodded and held onto Jesse.

Suddenly, a black tuxedo blocked her vision. She looked up and met the angry eyes of Will.

"Shit," she whispered.

"Why the hell did you leave us?" He growled at her and stepped closer. "Give me one reason to not have you removed right now."

She could no longer control herself or her tears. They slid down her face and she hiccupped. Her chest tightened with the fear of rejection teasing the air between them.

"There's no excuse for what I did. I got scared and fled. Everything happened so fast. I didn't know how to react to it. I'm so sorry. I'm here to ask for forgiveness and a second chance."

He sniffed the air, then leaned in and sniffed again.

Tawne leaned away from him and frowned. "Why are you sniffing me?"

"You smell different."

"Oh, that." She paused when Cristofano, Evan, and Chayton approached.

"I'm going to take my leave. Will you be okay?" Jesse asked.

"She'll be fine," Cristofano answered. "Thank you for escorting her."

Jesse nodded and backed away.

The men moved around Tawne and surrounded her, like a fawn stalked by four hungry lions. She swallowed against the dryness in her throat. "I don't know where to start."

Someone stood close behind her. They weren't touching her, but she could feel their presence. Was this part of the serum? She wouldn't have felt this before now.

She turned around and found Chayton leaning into her. He sniffed the air around her.

"You smell different."

"Same thing I said," Will told him.

"Did you take the serum?" Cristofano asked.

She nodded. "Yes, I did. Sasha came and picked me up and brought me here. We stopped on the way for the serum."

Chayton raised his brows. "How do you feel?"

"Different, but I haven't quite figured out how different. My senses are keener, that much I do know."

"Why did you leave?" Evan asked her.

"I got scared. So much happened so fast, it scared me. Nothing has ever happened so good like this for me. Everyone in my life has either left or died. Having four amazing men in my life that felt like they were made just for me, it frightened the life out of me."

"Did you consider how it would make us feel?" Cristofano asked.

She nodded. "I did, and it killed me inside."

"So, you want this then?" Will asked.

"Yes," she answered. "I want this life. I want all of you. I need you in my life." She shook her head and tried again. "I used to believe in one man and one woman. There was a soul mate out there for everyone, at least once. But, now, things are different. Before I met you, I felt like my soul was torn apart, ripped away and discarded. It was scattered all over the universe. The moment I met the four of you, I felt myself slowly becoming mended. When we finally had sex, everything I am became whole with the four of you. I am whole, I am home."

"For an eternity?" Will asked. His voice didn't sound so angry now. Maybe irritated, but at least more gentle.

She nodded. "All I ask is for you all to be patient with me while I adjust to all of this."

Chayton chuckled. "As if it will be a walk in the park with us having you around. We'll want you all the time, every day, when we have duties to tend to ourselves. I'm sure we'll manage with patience."

She laughed, then covered her mouth.

"You still have work with the coven if you want it?" Cristofano asked.

She nodded. "Yes, I'd love to."

"Then I think we're done here," Will said.

Cristofano nodded and held his hand out for hers. She accepted it and he pulled her to his side. "Welcome to our family, Tawne."

***

The broken are comforted by their own inner demons for so long, after a while, they forget what it feels like to be whole. The familiar claws of self-doubt have become part of their very being, that if they were removed, a part of their soul may shatter.

Tawne's soul shattered today. The

demons of self-doubt and loneliness no longer had a stake in her welfare. Liberation filled her and when she stepped through the door of her new home with her vampires, a squeal of triumph powered from her lungs.

She was home. She hadn't felt this in her heart since before her parents passing.

The doors closed behind her and she heard a few chuckles. Turning, she stood in the den's entrance. Vaulted ceilings with paintings on the walls, she kept her back to her men...for now.

"So, I believe she's made the right decision," Chayton called out.

"I do believe so," Evan answered.

She turned to face her four devastatingly handsome men. Each of them dressed in a tuxedo, they stood in a semi-circle around her. She kicked off her heels and her bare feet touched the cool hardwood floor.

"The question is," she retorted with a grin, "did you make the right call on me? Because the way I see it, you're stuck with me."

Cristofano smirked and removed his tux jacket, laying it on the backside of a sofa. "You drank the serum?"

She nodded. "I did."

"I'm glad you had a change of heart." Removing his jacket and lying next to Cristofano's, Will pushed his hands into his pockets. "I can't imagine this life with someone other than you."

She smiled. "Even after our rocky start?"

"Call it character development," he teased with a wink.

"Chayton," she called. "Since the serum was yours, I thought you should try the finished goods first."

He lifted a brow. "If I may be so bold, Miss O'Brien, there is much more I would like to do to you while tasting your blood."

Her knees weakened and as she took another step back, the back of her legs met the target she had aimed for, the dark gray chaise lounge. She sat down on it and kept her eyes trained on Chayton.

"What did you have in mind?" She licked her lips and her panties felt drenched with a need only her men could fulfill.

"I think we could have fun with this," he announced and reached for his tie. He removed it and stepped around the chaise.

She followed his movements until he was behind her. Turning her attention to the other three in front of her, she made a point to stare at the erections each of them had in their pants.

"Why don't you shed the clothes?" She smiled, then gasped when the black fabric of Chayton's tie lowered over her eyes.

"No peeking," he whispered in her ear.

She nibbled on her lower lip. Anticipation and excitement bubbled to the surface, along with a giggle.

A soft and gentle hand slipped around her neck and tilted her head back, laying her down on the chaise. Someone moved their mouth over hers and she instinctively knew it was Chayton. Capturing her lips for a brief moment, he peppered his way to her neck. A pair of hands slid up the inside of her thighs, then pushed her legs apart.

"Her panties are so wet," Will groaned. He flicked his finger over her clit and her hips bucked. The same hands tugged her panties down her legs. "Beautiful," he whispered just before his mouth pressed against her core. His tongue slid from her entrance to her clit, then back again.

"Holy hell," she whispered. "I need you inside me, please."

"Open your mouth," Chayton whispered. He slid his hands under her neck and tilted her head back. His cock pressed to the seam of her mouth and she opened it. Holding onto her head, he started out slow, pushing his dick further into her mouth with each stroke...until she'd had enough of the teasing.

She reached back for him and grabbed his thighs, then pulled him toward her.

"Fuck her mouth," Evan growled.

Taking the hint, Chayton thrust his cock harder into her mouth, causing her to gag and choke on his dick. The head of his cock hit the back of her throat and using both hands to grasp her cheeks, he held himself against her mouth. When he finally released her, she gasped and coughed, then swiped at her mouth.

He pushed his dick back in and held it in her throat once more. When she gagged, he groaned and released the hold he held on her.

Chayton wiped the spit on her face away. "That was beautiful," he told her.

"Thank you," she answered with a groan.

Will pulled her body toward him, his face burying further into her pussy. He sucked on her clit and teased her throbbing pearl between his teeth and his magnificent tongue.

"I'm going to fucking come, holy fuck!" Tawne screamed out and her back arched. She reached for Will, but someone grabbed her arms instead. Her legs spasmed and her hips bucked against his mouth. Then, her body shattered in a heart pounding orgasm.

"Shit!" she screamed. "Yes, holy mother of all things, yes!"

Will licked her once more, then pulled away. Her heart pounded, and her chest rose and fell with manic breaths. She reached for the blindfold when her arms were restrained.

"Why can't I use my arms?"

"You will, once we're ready for you to," Cristofano answered. "But, first, I need you to stand."

Whoever held her hands pulled her, and she stood to her feet. Her thighs were creamed from her orgasm and felt slick.

"Raise your arms," he told her.

She did so, and her dress was pulled up over her head. Her bra was removed as well. A mouth sucked on her nipple and a hand massaged the other one. Then from behind, someone pushed her ass cheeks apart and licked her puckered hole.

She had never had anyone do this, and honestly, it was hot. She moaned and bent over for more. Instead, lube dribbled over the slit of her ass and down her thighs. A finger pushed past the hole and moved in and out, slicking her tightness. Another finger joined the first, and scissor movements stretched her back channel.

"I'm going to pull you down to me," Cristofano told her. "When I do, you'll feel my cock penetrate that remarkable ass of yours."

She nodded and followed his movements. She lowered herself and felt his ridged manhood touch her back entrance. She wanted this from him, from all of them. His head pushed past the tight entrance. His hands gripped the sides of her hips and guided her down.

"Easy," he told her. "I don't want to hurt you."

"It doesn't hurt," she groaned. "Let me do this." A renewed confidence resonated in her and she gritted her teeth. She moved her ass up and down, slowly taking his cock deeper and deeper inside her. A moment passed when she felt relieved he was fully inside her. Tawne slid up and down on his hardness from the head of his cock down to the bottom of his shaft.

"Fuck, woman, your ass is so fucking tight," Cristofano growled.

"Lean back against him," Evan whispered next to her ear.

Tawne nodded and felt Cristofano hold her back, guiding until she leaned against his chest. He reached around her body and grasped her legs behind her knees, then pulled them to her chest.

When he thrust his cock into her ass once more, she screamed. He plunged deep inside her and hit the sensitive nerve endings, proving an orgasm as easily as pushing a button.

"Gods, her honey is dripping from her," Will groaned.

Cristofano thrust again, and like before, another orgasm shot through her body. Her legs shook, and her head relaxed against his shoulder.

"Fuck me, please!" she screamed.

Evan leaned over her and pressed his dick to her entrance then slid into her pussy. When he pushed in, Cristofano pulled out, forming a rhythm. Tawne groaned, every ounce of her body burning with desire. She had shattered and knew there was no going back.

Her arms were pulled to the sides and the pulse points over her wrists were licked on either side. At the same time, Cristofano licked her shoulder and Evan tongued over her left breast. All four of her men were now feeding on her and this provided a sensation that broke Tawne. She was ruined in the best possible way.

"Time to share," Cristofano growled in her ear, then licked her lobe.

"Help her to her feet and bring her to me," Chayton said.

Evan slid his lips over hers, his tongue fighting with hers for dominance. "My love," he whispered, then pulled free of her. He took her hands and helped her sit up.

Cristofano carefully extracted his cock from her ass and she stood. "I look forward to many nights of this." He pressed a kiss against her left ass cheek, then spanked the right side.

She grinned and took a few steps backward toward the chaise lounge. Her hands met another's, and she smiled. "Chayton?"

"Yes, my love," he told her. "Straddle me and allow me to fuck you."

She licked her lips and holding onto the couch, she straddled his hips and felt the head of his cock at her entrance. She slid down over his cock seating herself firmly against his hips.

"Bend over," she heard Will whisper beside her ear as his hand gently pressed against her back. More lube was smeared across her ass, then she felt his dick press against her hole, and then he pushed past the ring of muscle.

"Fuck," she groaned, and her forehead rested against Chayton's. Will lifted her right arm and licked at the inner elbow, then his fangs penetrated her skin.

"She tastes amazing, like liquid gold," Will announced.

Evan's soft, gentle hand cupped her face and turned her to the left. He pressed the head of his cock to her lips and she opened her mouth. She tasted herself on his dick and opened her throat for him to fuck her mouth.

"Can she feed from us," Cristofano asked and licked her inner elbow.

"Yes," Chayton groaned with a thrust into her pussy.

Will feathered his lips across her shoulder, then slowly pulled free from her backside. "Allow her to lie down. She needs to rest."

"She needs the hot tub," Cristofano

added.

Evan moved away from her mouth, his member softening.

Chayton held her body to his and when he stood, he laid her on her back, then pulled himself free. "Her blood is perfect now. She now needs to feed from us to heal. Or she will never want to do this again."

She stared into his brown eyes. "This won't change me into a vampire?"

He shook his head. "The blood that now courses through your veins is synthetic demon blood. Feeding from us acts like a bonding agent for your blood. It will help you rapidly heal and work in conjunction to keep you youthful. Trust me when I say you'll need it to heal."

She nodded with full trust. "Will you be first?" she asked.

"I would love to be," Chayton answered.

She heard what could only be

described as the sound of flesh being ripped, then a warm substance dripped onto her lips.

"Open your mouth, my love," Will told her.

She did, and an arm was pressed to her mouth. The blood pooled in her mouth and instinct made her want to fight, but the taste drove her in the complete opposite direction. She swallowed and pulled on his vein for more. It was sweet, like a warm chocolate sauce hinted with cinnamon.

He pulled his arm free and another was pressed to her mouth. Before long, all four men had fed their human, and the room grew quiet as she relaxed into the chaise and sleep teased at her mind.

Her body was scooped up into a set of strong arms. She leaned against the firm chest and when she opened her eyes, she realized Will held her.

She smiled up at him and then allowed

her lashes to drift closed again as slumber pulled her under so deep words from her men were inaudible to her ears.

Chapter Nineteen

A YEAR HAD passed since Tawne's new life began with her vampires. She took on the apprenticeship with the coven's current curator. She'd learned from their leaders about the artifacts, their history, and made a footprint in their history. Some of the old relics had become faded and with Tawne's help, they were becoming restored once more.

She'd volunteered to become the confidant to humans who were looking to commit to this change. She was more than just a human turned concubine, she was a human who had found her place in a new world where vampires ruled, and she'd become the universe to her vampires at home.

Chayton had already begun testing new serums to perfect what he had in place. He wanted to create the ability to change anyone, demon, shifter, human or otherwise, into a blood demon. With the serum working on humans, the sky was now the limit for any possible situation. It was simply finding the right combination. He only needed time to make it perfect, and when your life is an eternity, time could pass in the blink of an eye.

Will's clients had doubled in the year that had passed. He won most cases he supported, but the occasional ones that were lost, he wasn't too torn up over. When representing vampires hell bent on ruining human's lives, there's not much for support in their future.

Evan had continued his accounting with the coven and most days, met with Tawne during her time there. Stealing a kiss here or discussing artifacts there, she enjoyed seeing her men during her time working.

Cristofano invested and backed Chayton's practice. He'd recently met with Jared, and together both men had created a new company to begin the setup of future humans, demons, and concubines throughout the world. The warehouse district held its place in the world for quite some time, but the community of vampires continued to grow significantly.

They also needed a base headquarter location for one coven above all covens. New Orleans was the perfect prospect for such a location. Soon, the men would present this idea to the coven and, from there, a new home base would form. That was, of course, if their plans were approved. With their community growing at the rate it was, there was need for a government for their part of the world. Cristofano and Jared might begin to run things, but it didn't mean they wanted all that control. Who would become the new ruler of their world? In time, it would be determined. Until then, the men would enjoy their life with their human.

THE END

Watch for Book 3 in The Covenant of New Orleans series, The Succubus and Her Vampires...

About the Author

Hailing from Burleson, Texas, USA Today Bestselling Author Julie Morgan grew up in the country with big tractors and bonfire parties. She now resides in sunny Central Florida with her husband and daughter where she writes paranormal romance, contemporary romance (rock & roll, military), and dabbles in fantasy.

Where to Find More of Julie Morgan

Join Julie's newsletter, be the first to receive new book details, and receive a free book!

http://www.juliemorganbooks.com/newsletter.html

Facebook:

http://www.facebook.com/juliemorganbook

Twitter:

http://www.twitter.com/juliemorganbook

Also by Julie Morgan

Chronicles of the Fallen series

Fallen

Redemption

Atonement

Culmination

Rapture, a short story

Southern Roots series

Southern Roots

City Lights

Fueled Desire

Driven Hunger

Paramour

Playing Her Body

Deadly Alchemy series

Deadly Alchemy

Fatal Intentions

Wicked Alchemy

Special Ops series

Delta Force

Sniper

Ranger (coming soon!)

Seal (coming soon!)

The Covenant of New Orleans series

The Concubine and Her Vampires

The Human and Her Vampires

The Succubus and Her Vampires (coming soon!)

Stand Alone Books:

Dragon Master

Stone Obsession, The Cursed Seas Collection

Shared World

HOT SEALs: Guarded by a SEAL